A.W. Faber-Castell
The Magic Pencil 3

AF117520

The Magic Pencil 3
Copyright © 2022 by Castell Trading Pty Ltd

All rights reserved. No part of this publication may be reproduced, distributed, or transmitted in any form or by any means, including photocopying, recording, or other electronic or mechanical methods, without the prior written permission of the author, except in the case of brief quotations embodied in critical reviews and certain other non-commercial uses permitted by copyright law.

Tellwell Talent
www.tellwell.ca

ISBN
978-0-2288-5903-1 (Hardcover)
978-0-2288-5902-4 (Paperback)
978-0-2288-5904-8 (eBook)

I would like to gratefully acknowledge family, friends and colleagues who have contributed in many ways to bring my writing to fruition.

Author: Count Andreas Wilhelm von Faber-Castell

For author A.W. Faber-Castell (Count Andreas von Faber-Castell), every pencil holds the promise of magic. From the time he was a young boy he has always regarded pencils as small magic wands that inspire creativity and make the imagination visible.

Known as Count Andy to his colleagues, he is the last surviving member of the 8th generation pencil dynasty to have been actively involved in the running of the famous company, which began in Germany in 1761.

Andy was the company's undisputed champion for developing children's products – the main contributor to Faber-Castell's success over recent decades. One of his claims to fame was the launch of his beloved Connector Pen. He was its sole champion initially, but with passion and persistence he ultimately brought the disbelievers in the company on board. The pen became famous worldwide, and it has been the number one colouring product in Australia for the past twenty-five years.

Fritz the Painter

Hermann the Plumber

Rollover von Cracklingen

Werner Little Werner

Reverend Semmelmeier

Dr. Ulrich Folterknecht

Lucifer

Table of Contents

CHAPTER ONE 1
CHAPTER TWO 5
CHAPTER THREE 9
CHAPTER FOUR 13
CHAPTER FIVE 17
CHAPTER SIX 21
CHAPTER SEVEN 26
CHAPTER EIGHT 30
CHAPTER NINE 35
CHAPTER TEN 40
CHAPTER ELEVEN 42
CHAPTER TWELVE 44
CHAPTER THIRTEEN 48
CHAPTER FOURTEEN 53
CHAPTER FIFTEEN 57
CHAPTER SIXTEEN 61
CHAPTER SEVENTEEN 67
CHAPTER EIGHTEEN 70
CHAPTER NINETEEN 75
CHAPTER TWENTY 79

CHAPTER TWENTY-ONE 81
CHAPTER TWENTY-TWO 86
CHAPTER TWENTY-THREE 90
CHAPTER TWENTY-FOUR 94
CHAPTER TWENTY-FIVE 97
CHAPTER TWENTY-SIX 101
CHAPTER TWENTY-SEVEN 106
CHAPTER TWENTY-EIGHT 112
CHAPTER TWENTY-NINE 116
CHAPTER THIRTY 120
CHAPTER THIRTY-ONE 122

1

Time passes, but true friendship stays put. Even though young Andy wouldn't have expressed it that way, he knew instinctively that no matter how long he had to wait for the magic pencil to return, their friendship would be as strong as ever.

But it didn't make the waiting any easier. Andy was in a constant state of longing to see the pencil again. Every morning, for nine months, he crossed a number off his wall calendar as he counted down to the day he would once again hear the pencil's voice in his head. And now finally, at last, that exciting day had arrived!

Andy imagined that even his dog, Sassy, was excited by the prospect. He was pleased that she had recovered from her confusion after the magic pencil accidentally put the animal love spell on her. Sassy never felt good about it, but she eventually got used to the fact that every animal she met—domestic pets and wild creatures alike—loved her. It was impossible for her to chase any wild animals in the fields and forest because none ran away from her. Quite the reverse, in fact. Rabbits actually ran towards her for a cuddle, squirrels tried to feed her nuts and birds landed on her back. Even all the cats in the neighbourhood steadfastly rubbed their heads on her chest, purring loudly while totally ignoring her ferocious growling and barking. Cats not afraid of her! Outrageous! What was a fierce, red-blooded dog to do? If dogs could look embarrassed and humiliated, Sassy certainly did each time it happened.

'Don't worry, Sassy!' Andy would laugh. 'You're still the best dog a boy could have.'

To cheer her up on such occasions Andy would throw balls for her to fetch. And, as a special treat, Andy sometimes flew a little drone close to the ground, which she loved to chase. It quickly became her favourite game; at least it ran away from her!

'So, I hear you've been a very good boy while I was away and didn't use your special powers at all! Congratulations, Andy!'

Andy almost fainted on the spot as his head instantly began spinning with excitement at the sudden sound of that familiar voice inside it. Tears of joy welled in his eyes, before spilling over and running down his cheeks.

'Finally!' he sobbed. 'Finally, you are back! I don't want you to leave me ever again!'

'Don't worry, Andy, I'll be here for quite a while.'

Andy didn't like the sound of that at all. "Quite a while" didn't sound like "forever" to him.

'But, Mi—' He was about to blurt out the magic pencil's name when he cut himself short. It was only at the very end of the pencil's last visit that she told him her name. He was surprised it was Michaela, a girl's name. He'd never thought about whether the pencil was male or female; it was a disembodied voice in his head. He hadn't quite gotten used to the fact that it ... she ... had a name.

'It's OK to say my name, Andy,' the pencil said.

'It just feels weird,' Andy muttered, 'to call a voice in my head or a pencil in my pocket Michaela. Maybe if you were real, I could do it.'

'I am real, Andy.'

'Sorry ... yes, I know. I just meant if you were—'

'Human?' the magic pencil said.

'Umm ... yes, I guess.'

'Well, I do have a human form as Michaela, which I use when circumstances call for it.'

'Really?' Andy cried. 'Can you show me?'

'Of course, but only briefly. I'm not permitted by the spirit masters to take my human form without a very good reason and their consent in advance. They may instantly call me back if I transgress. I don't have their consent, but I do have a good reason, so I'll risk it. Just for a short time, though.'

At that, a very pretty dark-haired girl about Andy's own age materialised right before his eyes. She had olive skin and bright emerald-green eyes.

'Wow!' Andy cried, gawping.

'Hello, Andy.'

'H-h-h-hello ... Michaela.'

'You don't have to call me Michaela all the time—perhaps just on the rare occasions I'm in my human form. Otherwise, just talk to me as you have been doing.'

'OK, thanks,' Andy said. He sounded normal, but he had a very confused look on his face. 'Your voice has totally changed,' Andy said. 'You sound like a young girl.' Then he realised what a dumb remark it was and looked embarrassed.

'Only when I *am* a young girl, Andy,' the pencil replied without sarcasm.

'Yeah ... of course,' Andy muttered, embarrassed. But he quickly regained his confidence. 'By the way, what was the good reason you said you had for turning human?'

'Very good, Andy! You're getting better at listening! The reason is that I was going to tell you about one of the new skills I learnt while I was away at spirit boot camp—which was very harrowing, I must say.'

'What new skill?' Andy said excitedly, ignoring the pencil's appeal for sympathy. 'Tell me! Tell me!'

'You've just seen it, Andy,' Michaela said with a broad grin.

'What?'

'Materialisation!' Michaela said. 'I was able to show it to you rather than simply tell you about it.'

'Oh ... wow!' Andy cried. 'Do it again!' He suddenly realised what he had said and wished he hadn't.

'I was about to,' Michaela responded. At that, she dematerialised, vanishing into thin air.

'Incredible!' Andy cried. 'Now come back again.'

'No,' the magic pencil said, once again as just a voice in Andy's head and a magic pencil in his pocket. 'My humanisation time is up, for now.'

'But ... but ... can you materialise something else?' Andy pleaded. 'I want another demonstration!'

'Take the cap off my pencil and place me on the floor,' the magic pencil ordered, back to its normal, bossy self.

2

Andy placed the pencil on the floor, as he was told. A split second later he leapt up onto his bed in terror ... with Sassy jumping after him and bouncing off his chest. Right there before them was a monstrous, grouchy-looking tiger whose full-throated ferocious growling reverberated throughout the house.

Anna, who happened to be in the room opposite to Andy's, opened his door ready to scold her son for making such an awful noise. She almost fainted with fright when she saw the tiger's snarling face but somehow managed to stay on her feet. She staggered out of the room and stumbled down the stairs crying out for Johann.

'THERE'S A TIII ... THERE'S A TIII... a TIGER IN YOUR SON'S ROOM! DO SOMETHING, JOHANN!'

Johann swore under his breath and put his book down. Grabbing one of his walking sticks, just in case, he stormed up the stairs and into Andy's room. Learning what a useless weapon a walking stick would be against a fully-grown tiger was a lesson he, fortunately, didn't have to suffer. Half expecting to be confronted by a huge striped cat, all he saw was a small tabby kitten pouncing around Sassy, whose tail was wagging happily.

'Ahhh!' Johann muttered, grabbing the kitten and heading back downstairs. 'Anna! What is wrong with you? It's just a little pussycat. I didn't realise you'd allowed Andy to get one.'

The only response he got was some moaning coming from the kitchen. Johann shook his head in bemusement and settled back into his comfortable chair with the kitten on his lap. Before he had time to pick up his book and resume reading, the kitten turned into an enormous python. Now it was Johann's turn to shriek. 'Yahhhhhhh! The rotten cat is now a huge SN ... SN... SNAKE! I HATE SNAKES!' Johann leapt out of his chair, sending the python sliding across the floor. Before the snake came to rest, it turned into a tiny mouse.

'What is going on here?' he screeched. 'Andy!'

The sound of his screeching frightened the mouse. It took off, disappearing into the kitchen. The shriek from the kitchen made Johann's screech sound like a half-hearted yell. It was so loud and piercing that it shattered his reading glasses. The magic pencil could have turned itself into a crocodile or grizzly bear or any other wild beast, but it would not have had the same terrorising effect on Anna as the little mouse did.

Andy had come running down the stairs the instant Johann had screeched his name and ran straight into the kitchen. 'Mum! Mum! Are you OK?'

Anna couldn't speak. She was standing on a chair pointing frantically at the mouse on the floor below her.

'What? What?' Andy said. From the volume and hysteria of his mother's shrieks he half expected to see the tiger in the kitchen. Then he saw the mouse. 'Mum ... it's just a mouse.'

Anna barely managed to get three words out: 'Take ... it ... away!'

Andy plucked the mouse off the floor just as Johann burst in. 'What's going on?' he demanded.

At that moment, the mouse turned back into the magic pencil. 'Hello, Anna! Hello, sir!' it said. 'I'm back!'

'Oh, no!' gasped Johann. 'I knew it! I knew it! Disaster has returned! And it can turn into a snake of all things! I hate snakes!'

'A mouse is much worse!' Anna cried.

'Why are you afraid of something that can't hurt you?' asked a voice that wasn't Johann's or Andy's.

Johann and Anna looked around in astonishment to see a pretty dark-haired girl with striking green eyes sitting at the kitchen bench.

'Mum, Dad,' Andy said quickly. 'This is Michaela—the magic pencil in its human form.'

'I wouldn't let those animals hurt you,' Michaela said, trying to reassure Anna and Johann, unsuccessfully by the look on their faces.

'Can you change into anyone you want to—like Kunnikunde?' Andy asked excitedly.

'NO! Please don't!' Johann cried. 'In this case, I'd prefer a snake!'

'Don't worry, sir,' Michaela said. 'I couldn't perform Andy's silly suggestion even if I wanted to.' She spread both her arms out. 'The only human form I can adopt is this one ... and only for a limited period each time. During my recent return to the spirit world, my masters decided that the human form of a little girl would be the most effective for our purposes. But while I was gone, I did learn a lot about using psychic power and the manipulation of just about any material'—Michaela grinned mischievously—'including flesh and bones.'

At that, Johann suddenly shrank to half his normal size. His shock quickly turned to anger.

'What? What is this?' he shouted, looking around frantically and twisting on the spot. 'Little girl ... I'm really starting to dislike you! I much preferred you as just a—'

Before he could finish his sentence, he resumed his usual size.

'Wow!' Andy cried. 'Show me more!'

'Not now, my demanding friend. I need to rest for a couple of days.'

She wasn't the only one. Johann was slumped in a chair in a daze after his shrinking experience. He looked like he'd need a couple of weeks, not days, to rest and recover.

Michaela wasn't concerned, or apologetic, as she continued talking. 'Then we start preparing for our next journey. We only have three months to get organised—and we'll need every minute of it.'

With that, the spirit Michaela disappeared back into the magic pencil. 'This pencil is my home,' they all heard in the pencil's usual nondescript voice in their heads. 'And by the way, magic spirits are living in pencils all over the world. Not like me—I have a special purpose, a mission to protect you, Andy, and your parents. But all the other spirits living in pencils are creative spirits whose special purpose is to help inspire new ideas and develop great minds.'

Andy was bursting with questions for the pencil, but the moment he started to ask one, all he got was: 'Shhh! I need to rest!'

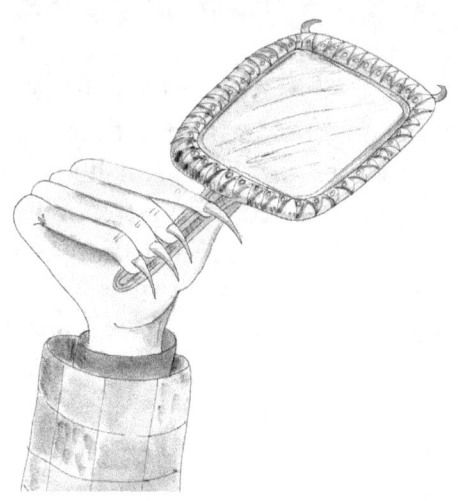

3

To Andy's great frustration, the pencil wasn't kidding—it was at least five days before it started chatting again. And when it did, it took Andy completely by surprise because he was right in the middle of a soccer match, leaping forward trying to score a goal. His shot just brushed the outside of the goal post.

'A couple of extra steps to the left would have put you in the perfect position to shoot and greatly increased your chance to score,' scolded the pencil.

'Thanks for the tip,' Andy responded sarcastically in his thoughts. 'Great timing ... *after* I'd just kicked the ball! Besides, I didn't have time to do small steps.'

'Yes, you did. Small, nimble steps in this case would have been far more effective than clumsy leaps forward! It's the same in real life,' the pencil insisted. 'Many small steps are better than a giant leap. Attempting a giant leap from the start makes your chances of falling much more likely.'

'OK! OK! Next time, I'll try nimble little steps!' Despite his annoyance at the pencil's unwanted advice about how to kick a soccer ball, nothing could ruin Andy's delight that the pencil was back chatting with him. He still had all the questions he'd wanted answered five days ago, so the two of them talked for a long time about all kinds of things. Andy just kept firing questions at the pencil, which refused to answer most of them.

Later, after the soccer game had finished, Andy's anger was starting to show when he asked the pencil about religion. 'So, tell me,' he demanded of the pencil, rather than merely asking him. 'Are all our religious beliefs wrong?'

'Why are you sounding so aggressive, Andy?' the pencil asked.

'Because I know you know the answers to my questions, but you won't tell me! Especially one question!'

'Which question?'

'You know which one!'

'What happens when you die?'

'Yes!' Andy yelled, almost in tears with frustration.

'I have told you a lot about life as a spirit already, Andy,' the pencil said, its tone softening out of respect for Andy's feelings. 'Two years ago, I even went beyond my authorisation. You know that when you believe something you can never prove is true, it's called faith. Believing something doesn't make it a fact.

'But a religion that preaches harmony among people and all living things can't be wrong, Andy. A religion that builds up a society to care and share can't be wrong. A religion that demands of you that you behave like a decent human being and resist the devil's temptation can't be wrong.

'I could go on, but I won't. Everyone needs to believe and dream. Your dream is your fantasy and your imagination. If they are not part of your life, your existence will become empty. Even if you can't always know, you can dream. You can't know what will happen after you die, but you can dream about how you would like it to be.'

'OK! OK!' Andy spluttered, trying not to raise his voice as he had done before. 'But I'd prefer to know.'

'You will know when you reach that path, Andy. And you will, like everybody else, because death is inevitable. We spirits call it the crossover—from the body to the spirit. In fact, you should rather look forward to it ... especially you, Andy, because you know so much more about the spirit world than other people, thanks to me.

'Part of you is already a spirit, Andy ... your soul. You have a good soul, so you can live a full, rewarding life with that good spirit inside you.'

'So, I'm already partly like you, partly a spirit?' Andy asked, excited by the idea. 'I'd never thought of my soul that way before!'

'It's true,' the magic pencil said. 'But remember, you are in charge of your own life until your body dies; no one else is. And the better life you live in your body, the better spirit you will be. And that will also help you choose wisely when you reach the crossover point.'

'When I die, you mean?'

'Yes. You have to choose wisely; don't ever let your good spirit be damned by the temptations and tricks of the devil.'

What a lecture! Andy thought. But at the same time, the pencil had opened his eyes to things he had never considered before. And he came to terms with the fact that there are things human beings would never know and that death is a crossover, a new beginning and not the end.

'Now, Andy, no more questions!' the pencil said, quite unreasonably given his next remark. 'We have a lot of preparations to make before he arrives.'

Naturally, Andy had another question to ask: 'Who's "he"?'

'Lucifer—the devil himself! The source of all evil; the dark angel of chaos, war and destruction; the being you humans call Satan.' The pencil's voice rose with passion and intensity. 'The King of Darkness! Diabolo! The personification of pure evil! The most powerful evil spirit of the entire cosmos! With his army of fiendish demons, he tries to take as many souls as possible over to the dark side and into the fiery abyss of hell! He's the incarnation of bad!'

If the magic pencil really wanted Andy to stop asking questions, this was not the way to do it. Andy was getting scared. 'What can we do? Can we stop him? How can we defeat this evil?'

'We can stop evil for a while, but we cannot defeat it completely.'

Andy looked aghast. 'So, we are all doomed!'

'No, no, Andy' the pencil replied. 'Evil will never defeat good, either. Good will always prevail—but at a cost.'

'But could the devil just come over to our house and kill us all?' Andy cried.

'Calm down, Andy. No, the devil is still a spirit, even though he can take the form of a human. He cannot kill directly, but he can induce other flesh-and-blood spirits to kill for him.'

'Devil's assassins!' Andy exclaimed, remembering something he'd read.

'Yes, I suppose you could call them that,' the pencil conceded. 'Lucifer could capture you but not kill you.'

'Oh,' Andy said. 'Then we have to watch out for my Aunt Kunnikunde. She's a devil's assassin—she's already tried to murder me once!'

'And she'll try again,' the pencil replied.

Oh, great! Andy thought.

'But I have a plan!' the pencil declared vehemently. 'It's a very carefully prepared plan for how to protect you, your family, your friends, and all the people of Stone as well. It will also free the three good spirits the devil has imprisoned in his magic mirror, which he carries around with him at all times when he's in human form. We have to get that mirror from him.'

4

Andy didn't think taking the devil's magic mirror from him would be too difficult. 'Ha! That's easy!' Andy exclaimed with the brash over-confidence of youth. 'I'll give him a karate kick to his knee, grab the mirror and run away!'

'Don't be an idiot, Andy,' the pencil snapped. 'With his super-speed, he would easily catch and imprison you as well. Until I teach you how to teleport yourself properly, you have no chance against him. And even then, you would have to be very lucky to escape his clutches.'

'Teleporting? Excellent!' Andy cried. 'And what other extra superpowers are you going to give me?'

'None!' the pencil retorted. 'However, I will make it possible for you to teleport yourself a thousand metres instead of just telehopping three metres at a time as you do now.'

That seemed to satisfy Andy's normally insatiable desire for more powers; he started to imagine how much fun it would be teleporting himself a thousand metres. But he didn't get time to think about it because, a split second later, the magic pencil turned into Michaela. She grabbed Andy's hand, dragging him away from the soccer field towards his home, announcing that they needed to talk to his parents right away.

The moment they were inside the house, Andy's mother began shaking her finger at Michaela. 'Never, ever turn yourself into a mouse again!' she commanded adamantly.

'And if you ever turn yourself into a snake again,' Johann declared crossly, 'I'll spank you—with a run-up!'

Anna and Johann's scolding of Michaela seemed to be more expressions of fear than anger.

'Don't be afraid, Anna and Johann,' Michaela said. 'It was just an experiment to test my newly acquired skills.'

'Bah!' Johann grunted. 'I much preferred you being the spirit voice in the magic pencil talking in our heads, rather than a young girl giving us orders.'

'With all due respect, sir,' Michaela responded, 'in our world, there is no age. The fact that I chose a young girl's form to adopt whenever I crossover doesn't mean my spirit knowledge and skills are any less than if I had chosen an adult's form. My spirit knowledge and powers are far superior to yours—and those of any living being—as you well know from our previous journeys.'

Johann nodded silently, if grumpily. Of course, he knew and appreciated the pencil's incredible powers. He just liked to make a fuss and sound off occasionally. And as the head of his own business, he wasn't used to taking orders—especially from a little girl!

'I will always be the magic pencil—it's my home,' Michaela went on. 'Pencils are where creativity lives! As we speak, there are billions of creative spirits living in both graphite and coloured pencils, sparking the imagination of children and adults the world over. They are not fully magic pencils like me; their magic is especially devoted to enhancing the creative power in people's minds and transferring that power through people's hands to their paper.'

Johann had no argument with this. He was as passionate about pencils as the magic pencil seemed to be. But it did get Johann thinking about how he went about marketing his pencils. *Maybe I should focus more on selling the fun, creativity and satisfaction our products provide, rather than on the actual pencil itself. Perhaps people buy the promise of the benefit the product offers, not the physical product for its own sake. Yes, that will be our new marketing mantra,* he thought. *People buy benefits, not products.*

Johann couldn't resist asking the magic pencil a question that for him was a very important one. 'In these modern times, why do creative spirits choose to make their homes in pencils rather than computers?'

'A very good question, sir!' the pencil said. 'It's true that devices such as computers, tablets and laptops are a crucial part of human life these days. They feed people with information and entertainment and provide global communication … and you can even write and draw with some of them. But the most creative writing and drawing don't come through a mechanical device like a keyboard or stylus, rather they flow much more effectively and smoothly directly from the mind to the hand and onto the paper via a pencil or pen. That amazing collaboration is what produces the most creative thinking and images.'

Johann was delighted with the answer Michaela had given him and immediately began to feel more comfortable in her presence. He started to think of her as a pencil soulmate.

Michaela, though, was focusing on other things. She led Johann, Anna and Andy to the lounge room to explain the new threat they were about to face. 'Lucifer, the devil himself, is coming to Stone,' Michaela said.

This was not what Johann wanted to hear and he sounded off in a typical fashion. 'Why is that every year, at about this time, some sort of great disturbance strikes?' he wailed. 'When will this all end so life can get back to normal? When … when?'

'Unfortunately, sir,' Michaela said, 'I can tell you that after this third episode there will be several more … three more, at least.'

Johann groaned loudly but said nothing.

'These episodes will recur until Kunnikunde is finally defeated.'

This was too much for Johann. 'Why did Arthur marry that woman?' he wailed. 'Why?'

Michaela's answer was cold and blunt. 'He didn't. She married him!'

Johann accepted this without comment and a long discussion ensued about what it would take to stop Satan from damaging Stone and terrorising its citizens.

Once the discussion had ended, Michaela turned back into the magic pencil and announced that she had started working on a plan that would safeguard everyone against the Evil One and his demons.

'By the way,' the pencil said, 'in conceiving a plan, my creativity was greatly enhanced resting in the point of the pencil.'

5

As he left his parents and returned to his room, Andy was feeling quite conflicted. On the one hand, he had his magic pencil back, but on the other, he missed the pretty Michaela, who could almost be his sister.

While he was grappling with this conflict, his mood suddenly turned to shock when the pencil calmly announced that it needed to leave again to collect material not available on Earth.

'Unfortunately,' the pencil said, 'your planet is ill-equipped to build a trap to capture Satan. I will have to beam the materials down from what you call the heavens in order to build a big barn for your father's sixtieth birthday.'

'Oh, yes,' Andy lamented, 'my father is getting very old!'

'Don't worry, Andy,' the pencil said. 'Your father is not so old! He has at least another thirty-seven years to live … if we can stop Kunnikunde from killing him, that is.'

'Oh, we have to!' Andy cried. 'Even though my mum is much younger, I don't think she would survive if Dad wasn't around.'

'I know,' the pencil said. 'Now, I have to go. I'll be gone for only about two weeks this time, Andy. But in the meantime, try to keep your father and mother away from the big area of lawn beside your driveway. That's where the special materials will appear when I beam them down. We don't want anyone on the lawn when they suddenly arrive!'

With that, a blue light burst from the pencil and Andy's friend was gone. Even though he had been warned, Andy was still devastated, and he knew the next two weeks would seem like an eternity. But he did his best to make the time go quickly by focusing on his schoolwork and playing with his friends Jurgen, Hansi and Hartmuth.

Focusing on his schoolwork was the hardest part, but the effort paid off; before he knew it, the two weeks had passed. Early one morning, he was overjoyed to hear the words, 'Wake up, sleepy head! We have work to do!'

Andy jumped out of bed. 'You're back! At last!' He snatched up the pencil from his bedside table, almost dropping it in his excitement.

'Careful!' the magic pencil said.

'Sorry!' Andy cried. 'What are we going to do now?'

'You're going to get dressed and have some breakfast. Then, before you go to school, you're going to take me to the machinery shed and leave me there until you come home.'

'Can't you use your magic and make me look sick, so I don't have to go to school?' Andy asked desperately.

'No,' the pencil replied sternly. 'I have a lot to do, and you can't help. And I must work in the daytime because the bright blue flashes I'll be creating will be far less visible than they would be at night.'

'But I've still got another six weeks before the summer holidays begin,' moaned Andy. 'I won't be able to see you during all that time!'

'Six weeks is perfect timing,' the pencil said. 'That's when I expect the devil and Kunnikunde to arrive. And one week after that is your father's birthday party.'

'We must make sure they don't ruin Dad's birthday party,' Andy said. 'What kind of weapons do you have? Can I have a gun to fight Kunnikunde and Satan?'

'Don't be silly, Andy! Guns aren't going to be any use against those two. Besides, the weapons I have are far superior to simple Earth weapons.'

'How do they work?' Andy asked excitedly.
'You'll find out soon enough.'

Every morning for the next five weeks, Andy dropped the magic pencil off in the machinery shed then picked him up again after school from exactly the same spot he had left him. Each time he looked around but saw no changes in the shed. He couldn't help wondering if the pencil was just lying there all day doing nothing. And the pencil was in no mood to chat, simply saying it had to think and focus. Andy's impatient curiosity turned to frustration and then anger. One morning, as the deadline rapidly approached, he finally exploded.

'There are only three days before my holidays start!' he shouted at the pencil. 'Three days before Kunnikunde and the devil arrive! Just ten days before my father's birthday! And you have done nothing! Nothing at all! You're even too lazy to talk to me!' Andy had tears of frustration and anger in his eyes.

'Andy! Andy!' the pencil responded, holding its own anger in check because it could understand Andy's frustration. 'Haven't I taught you that even the smallest creation, the simplest product needs imagination to make it a reality? Without an idea ... without a carefully thought-out plan ... nothing can happen! Imagination ... insight ... inspiration ... that's what leads to new inventions. They break through conventional thinking and produce great developments! They even drive the evolution of you human animals!'

'I'm not just an animal, like a dog or something! I'm a human being!' Andy shouted.

'So, your dog, Sassy, is "just an animal," not a being?' the pencil retorted.

'Of course, she's not! She's a ... she's a ... dog being!'

It was the first time Andy had heard the pencil laugh and he didn't like it. 'What's so funny?' he yelled.

'Let's stop here,' the pencil said soothingly. 'Trust me, Andy, as you always have before. I've been working very hard thinking. I need just one more day before I can implement my plan. Then you'll know everything. Have patience, my friend.'

The pencil's placating tone calmed Andy down somewhat. He decided he could cope with just one more day before his magic friend would be back to normal.

The next morning Andy awoke to find Michaela sitting at his desk.

'Good morning, sleepyhead,' she said brightly.

'Michaela!' Andy blurted out, delighted. He leapt out of bed, dragged a spare chair across to his desk and sat beside her. 'What are you doing?'

'Drawing up plans,' she said, not looking up.

Andy's eyes widened with astonishment. He couldn't believe the incredible speed she was drawing at. It only took Michaela a second or so to fill a complete page with an intricate drawing and detailed handwritten instructions.

'That's unbelievable!' Andy cried.

'What is?' Michaela said without breaking her rhythm.

'How fast you're drawing and writing.'

'Oh, that ... it's just my normal speed writing and speed drawing.'

'Wow! Can you teach me to do it?'

'No!' Michaela replied curtly.

'You're still in a really bad mood, aren't you?' Andy retorted, a little miffed.

Michaela stopped drawing and looked at him. 'I think you've forgotten who was in a bad mood. I wasn't the one doing all the shouting yesterday in the machinery shed.'

'Oh ... OK,' Andy muttered, partly repentant. 'Well ... you seem very grumpy.'

'If,' Michaela retorted sharply, 'trying to protect you and your family, and the whole population of Stone for that matter, from Satan himself is what you call grumpy, then so be it!'

Andy looked suitably chastised. 'Sorry,' he mumbled.

'Get ready! Get dressed!' Michaela commanded. 'We have work to do. Time is short!'

6

While Andy was getting dressed, Michaela turned back into the magic pencil. Andy put the pencil in his pocket and hurried downstairs for a quick breakfast. Ten minutes later he was in the machinery shed excitedly firing questions at the pencil. 'What's the plan? What are you going to do today?' Should I leave you here and go to school? What do you want me to do?'

'What I want you to do, Andy, is to stop asking questions and just listen carefully. No, you won't go to school today. It's the last day before the holidays and you won't miss much. And you won't be missed either because I've sent hypnotic thoughts to your teachers, so they'll believe they saw you at school today. Hide your schoolbag behind the tractor. Your father is at work, but make sure your mother doesn't see you until school is out.'

Andy was over the moon! Action at last! 'What can I do? What can I do?'

'As I just told you,' the pencil said, 'listen carefully. I'm going to teach you how to progress from telehopping to teleporting.'

'Wow! Yes!' Andy exclaimed, punching the air with both fists.

'Teleporting is far more difficult because you have to clearly envisage the place you'll be landing in.'

At that point, the pencil turned into Michaela again.

'I'll explain it all in more detail later,' she said. 'First I need some of the materials I've beamed down from outer space.'

Andy's curiosity was at a fever pitch. Every day for nearly six weeks, he had lamented to Michaela and constantly checked out the big lawn area beside the driveway for any sign of heavenly materials but had seen nothing whatsoever.

'I'm surprised you didn't look in the secluded lane next to the lawn, behind the thick bush,' Michaela said, a glint in her eye.

'Dad found a huge snake in those bushes a little while ago and told everyone to stay away from there until his forest man returned from holidays and removed it.'

Michaela grinned broadly, her startling green eyes sparkling. 'Yes, I took the form of a big red snake and made sure your father saw me last time he was walking in the lane. With his snake phobia, I knew he wouldn't be going back to the lane in a hurry. And I knew he wouldn't want others taking the risk either. Since this event is meant to be a surprise, I didn't want anyone to see the materials I'd placed there—especially not your father.'

When Andy entered the lane behind the bushes, he was astounded to find a massive collection of materials—wood planks and beams, roof tiles, steel bars and lots of cement bags. There were also several small bags containing different kinds of small smooth stones. But he couldn't see any extraordinary or unusual materials that couldn't be bought from the local building supplies store. There certainly wasn't anything that looked like it might have been beamed down from outer space.

'So,' Andy asked, a little disgruntled, 'what's so special about this stuff?'

'Wait and see. Pick up one of the small bags of pebbles and bring it to the machinery shed.'

Andy tried to oblige, but he found the bag so heavy he couldn't lift it off the ground.

'This is ridiculous!' he exclaimed as he grunted and groaned, trying to pick up the small bag. 'There are only a few pebbles in here! I should be able to pick it up easily!'

Enjoying Andy's futile efforts, Michaela made a show of rolling her eyes then calmly walked over and picked up the bag, easily, with one hand. She then picked up a second bag with her other hand and, shaking her head, carried them both off to the shed.

They are extremely heavy pebbles! Andy told himself as he stomped off after her. *I don't think you can buy those locally.*

'How did you do that?' he asked as soon as they were inside the shed.

'Levitation,' Michaela answered, 'the art of eliminating your Earth's gravity.' She waited for Andy's inevitable question.

'Can you teach me to do that?'

'NO!' was her inevitable answer. 'At least, not yet,' she added. 'You are already a kind of superman with all the powers I've given you. My spirit masters think I might have been a bit too free and easy with them. So, beyond teleportation, I'm not authorised to pass on any more special skills to you, unless a situation makes it absolutely necessary.'

Andy grunted his disappointment but kept his thoughts to himself.

Michaela carefully laid three of the pebbles out on the floor of the shed. 'I'll need these later this afternoon,' she explained. 'But first, we have to briefly visit Kunnikunde's castle.'

'That won't be easy,' Andy muttered, shaking his head. 'It's heavily guarded.'

Michaela smiled. 'That's why I'm going to teach you teleportation. A crucial part of the art is to know the exact spot you want to end up.' She produced a floor plan of the castle. 'Carefully study the layout of the castle and note precisely where Kunnikunde's bedroom is.'

Andy thought that was easy enough and after a few minutes looking at the plans he declared he was ready to go.

'Right!' Michaela said. 'Put me in your pocket.'

'What? How am—'

Michaela instantly turned back into the magic pencil.

'Oh ... yes,' Andy said, picking the pencil up and sliding it into his shirt pocket.

'Now,' the pencil ordered, 'focus intently on where Kunnikunde's bedroom is in the castle.'

Andy adopted a look of intense concentration ... well, his idea of one anyway.

Michaela seemed unimpressed. 'Andy! I said to focus, not stare blankly into space.'

'I'm focusing! I'm focusing!'

Seconds later ... WHOOSH! ... They were inside the castle. Unfortunately, Andy had focused on the wrong room. He'd teleported himself to Kunnikunde's office instead of her bedroom. He materialised right behind Mr Werner Little Werner, who was busily preparing plans for the imminent arrival of his beloved boss.

'Quick, Andy!' the pencil commanded. 'Take me out of your pocket and place me on the floor!'

Andy obliged, just in time. Sensing someone behind him, Werner spun around. His dumbfounded expression quickly turned into an evil grin as he eagerly grabbed a pistol that was on the desk beside him. With a yelp of glee, he stretched his arm out and aimed the gun at Andy, ready to fire. At that moment, the pencil turned into Michaela again. One glance at her by Werner was enough; he immediately went rigid, as if he were frozen.

'Instant hypnosis, Andy,' Michaela explained to a confused Andy. 'Works best on simple minds!'

As Michaela walked up to Werner, Andy saw two bright blue flashes. He watched her calmly take Werner's outstretched arm and drag it down so that his pistol was aiming directly at his big toe.

'Let's telehop next door, Andy,' Michaela said.

Thankfully, the room they landed in was empty. Seconds later a shot rang out, followed by an ear-piercing scream of pain. Not long after, a different screaming sound filled the air as an ambulance raced up to the front door of the castle.

'Just stand clear of the centre of the room, Andy. I'm going to teleport a bag of those special pebbles here.'

A WHOOSH later and the bag materialised before them. Andy telehopped from room to room with Michaela and watched her hide a pebble in each room. When they reached Kunnikunde's master bedroom with its huge fireplace, Michaela placed seven white pebbles in the grate. Andy tried to help but he could barely lift even the smallest pebble. He couldn't believe something so small could be so heavy.

Michaela took Andy's hand. 'I'll do the teleporting this time, Andy.'

7

Before Andy could even blink, they were back in the machinery shed. This was the moment he had a little meltdown. He sat on the floor as his body started to shiver all over; he couldn't stop it.

'That was scary!' he cried. 'I could have been killed by Mr Little Werner!'

'Not on my watch,' Michaela casually replied. 'But I did wonder why you just stood there when he pointed the gun at you and didn't use your telehopping skills.'

'I was so in awe of my new teleportation ability that I forgot I could also telehop out of the room!'

'Let this be a lesson to you,' Michaela said sternly. 'With the fright you've just experienced, I doubt you'll make that mistake again.'

Andy's shivering began to abate, and he got up off the floor. As soon as he had recovered fully, he started asking questions about the pebbles they had hidden all over the castle.

'They are really just to aggravate Satan and, hopefully, make him angry,' Michaela replied. 'They could do terrible damage to minor devils and demons, but they will just be irritants to the devil himself; sort of like mosquitos are to you, Andy. But they could make him itch all over and really annoy him.'

'But why do you want to irritate the devil?'

'To put him off his guard,' Michaela explained. 'Those pebbles are something only minor spirits would use to try to upset him. So hopefully he will assume that's what he's up against and underestimate us. No more questions for now. Go outside and wait until I tell you to come back in.'

'But why do I have to—'

'"No more questions," I said.' Michaela rolled her eyes. 'I have to build some tools to use against Satan. The intense flashes their construction will produce could be damaging to your eyesight. Now—outside!'

A short while later, Andy observed numerous bright blue flashes lighting up the windows of the shed. Suddenly a dazzling beam of light shot out of the disused chimney straight up into the sky. That surprised him enough, but what happened next made him almost jump out of his skin. Four distinct lightning strikes, one after another, exploded out of the sky and straight into the shed's chimney. For a second the whole shed turned blue, momentarily blinding Andy.

A minute later Michaela called out for him, and Andy stumbled towards the shed, still slightly dazed. Inside, he saw his magic friend standing admiring three small objects lying on a workbench. A closer look revealed a paintbrush, a hammer and a pencil with a silver protective cap—exactly the same as the one the magic spirit lived in.

Andy gasped with sheer disappointment. 'These are no weapons!' he exclaimed. 'Just some tools and a pen!'

Michaela smiled. 'Looks can be deceiving. They could be the most powerful tools you've ever seen. Now, look at me—what do you see?'

Andy looked closely at her, still hoping to detect the super weapons he expected after all the spectacular blue flashes and lightning strikes. 'I can't see anything special!' he loudly proclaimed, almost shouting in his frustration.

'Typical boy!' Michaela retorted, rolling her eyes. 'Your brain seems to be made out of banana peels! Look closer.'

As much as Andy strained his eyes, he couldn't see anything special.

'My dress, you idiot! Can't you see that it's a bit different and unusual?'

'Oh, yeah, you've put on a new dress. Big deal!'

'AAAARRRGH!' Michaela wailed. She turned this way and that on the spot a couple of times like a fashion model on a catwalk. 'I'm wearing a beautiful silky white dress with a fitted white jacket and silver shoes.'

'Very pretty,' Andy said, trying not to sound sarcastic.

'This outfit is the most amazing device I've ever constructed!' Michaela declared vehemently. 'It's made from some of the rarest materials in all the universes! It is a cloaking device against the devil's scan. Wearing this, I should be able to stand right in front of him without being detected as a spirit.'

'Oh, right,' Andy remarked, trying to share Michaela's excitement but still not convinced. He would much rather have seen some amazing out-of-this-world super weapon.

'Now, quickly,' Michaela said brusquely, 'let's get the hammer and paintbrush to Hermann the plumber and Fritz the painter and give them some magic! And you, Andy, will need a new jacket.'

With that, Michaela simply touched Andy's old hunting jacket and his whole appearance changed dramatically. His jacket, leather trousers and highly polished shoes looked brand new.

'Oh no!' he cried, looking down at his clothes. 'I look like a little fancy-pants snob in designer clothes! This is not my brand!'

'Stop griping, cry baby!' Michaela commanded. She picked up the replica pencil she had constructed. 'I want to see this pencil sticking out of your front pocket at all times! Understood?'

Andy nodded. 'Understood.'

'Now, we have work to do!' Michaela ordered. 'Pick up the hammer and paintbrush and let's go!'

Andy tried to pick the hammer up first but grunted with the effort; he could hardly lift it off the workbench.

Having had her fun at Andy's expense, Michaela touched Andy on the arm, and he could suddenly lift the hammer as if it were a pencil.

'How come it's now so light?' Andy asked, astonished.

'Well, cry baby,' she explained, 'I've made you fifty times stronger than you were before.'

'Wow!' Andy cried. 'Like Superman!'

'Not quite,' Michaela groaned. But then her tone became very serious. 'You are not to show off your increased strength,' she told him sternly. 'Especially in these next six days. The devil must think he's only up against minor spirits and ordinary human beings.'

'Of course ... whatever you say,' Andy replied, as he walked over to the tractor parked on the far side of the big shed. He grabbed the front of the machine under the radiator with one hand and easily lifted the front wheels off the floor. He punched the air with his other hand. 'I'm Superboy!' he shouted.

'Super stupid boy, more like it!' an angry Michaela shouted back. 'What did I just tell you?'

'Sorry! Sorry!' Andy cried, dropping the tractor, which bounced on its front tires twice before coming to rest. He raised both hands defensively. 'I just couldn't help testing my newfound gift. It's awesome!'

8

After giving Andy a terse dressing down, Michaela teleported them both to Hermann and Fritz's house in Stone. When he handed the hammer over to Hermann, Andy pretended it was extremely heavy. But the magic Michaela had given the hammer meant Hermann could pick it up as if it were a feather. He swung it around and declared that it felt good and well-balanced. Both Hermann and Fritz promised to help after noon the following day to erect the big barn needed to celebrate Johann's sixtieth birthday.

'Dad's away on business,' Andy explained, 'and he won't be back till the morning of his birthday.'

The next teleporting stop was the catering company, where Michaela produced a list of everything needed for the birthday celebration. Half an hour later, the catering manager told them it would cost ten thousand dollars.

'And how do you wish to pay?' he asked.

Andy was about to say he would get a cheque from his mother when Michaela piped up. 'We'll pay cash.'

Andy was taken aback. He turned to look at Michaela. Below the counter, out of sight of the manager, he saw thousand-dollar notes shoot from Michaela's right hand into her left, one after another, like a casino croupier dealing cards. 'I'm giving you eleven thousand dollars,' she said to the manager. 'One thousand extra to cover any additional costs.'

Andy, astonished, stood wide-eyed, impressed by how Michaela could produce money with a flick of her hand. He wanted to ask if she could teach him that, but he didn't dare. *Maybe later.*

Michaela performed the same trick at the florist after ordering many large flower bouquets.

Business concluded, Michaela gave Andy a chance to practice his teleporting skills. 'Why don't you teleport us back to the machinery shed,' she suggested.

'OK!' Andy said, excited at the prospect.

'Remember, Andy, focus carefully, as I've taught you.'

'Right,' Andy replied.

An instant later they found themselves in the thorn bushes next to the shed.

'Ow! Ow! Yah! Yowch!' Andy screamed as he fought his way out of the bushes. He didn't stop to think he could have telehopped out and saved himself a lot of pain.

'Bravo, Andy!' Michaela cried, clapping her hands with mock applause. 'Missed by *that* much!'

Andy was too distracted to respond. He was sucking a bleeding scratch on the back of one hand and trying to extract a thorn from his neck with the other.

Michaela wasn't showing any sympathy. 'What was your last thought before teleportation?'

'Yowch!' Andy cried as the thorn in his neck finally came out. 'I was thinking of your hand producing all that money.'

'You can't half-focus when you're teleporting, Andy.'

'OK, I'll remember next time,' he wailed, as he started to take his jacket off.

Michaela went ballistic. 'STOP! Don't you dare take your jacket off! For the next coming days, you will sleep in those clothes. You're not even to take your shoes off! These clothes you hate so much are a cloaking device to shield you against the devil's scan. If you were to wear normal clothes, he would immediately realise that you had become empowered! He would trap you and then systematically take every power you have away!'

'I would just telehop out of his trap,' Andy declared confidently.

'NO! NO! NO!' Michaela yelled. 'You cannot get out of the devil's trap. And for us to trap him instead, we will need the highest discipline, focus ... and luck! You must not take those clothes off until I say you can. Got it?'

'Got it,' Andy muttered. 'But I'm going to be pretty smelly and scruffy after one week!'

'No, you won't,' Michaela said in a calmer tone. 'The clothes are self-cleaning and wrinkle-free.' She rolled her eyes. 'In fact, you'll be a lot cleaner than your one-minute showers make you—when you bother to take one, that is.'

'Very funny,' Andy retorted grumpily.

'Under no circumstances are you to remove those clothes until I say so!'

'OK! OK! I won't!'

Once again, Michaela tried to make it clear to Andy that he was not to use his enhanced powers unless she ordered him to do so. 'We don't want any impulsive reactions or reckless initiative in this operation, Andy. You must stick precisely to my instructions.'

She formed a cross with the index finger of each hand. 'This will be the sign I will give you meaning the devil is present. At that moment there must be absolutely no communication between us—even in our thoughts. Is that clear?'

Andy nodded repeatedly without comment. He was finally beginning to understand just how serious the project was and how dire the circumstances would be if they failed.

Back at Andy's place, Michaela went through the entire house putting all valuables and other precious items out of sight in cupboards or locked in display cases behind glass. She also told Andy to place two heavy silver goblets on top of the dining room cabinet.

'Place one of them right on the corner's edge,' she instructed.

'Why are we doing all this?' Andy asked.

'We have to Kunnikunde-proof the house.'

Andy was aghast. 'Kunnikunde is coming here?"

'That's the plan,' Michaela replied. She paused and gazed into the distance beyond the room. 'Speak of the devil,' she said.

'Why?' Andy said.

'At this very moment, the devil and your demonic aunt, the evil countess, have materialised in the courtyard of Kunnikunde's castle right here in Stone.

'What?' Andy cried. 'What are we going to do?'

'Wait,' was Michaela's calm reply.

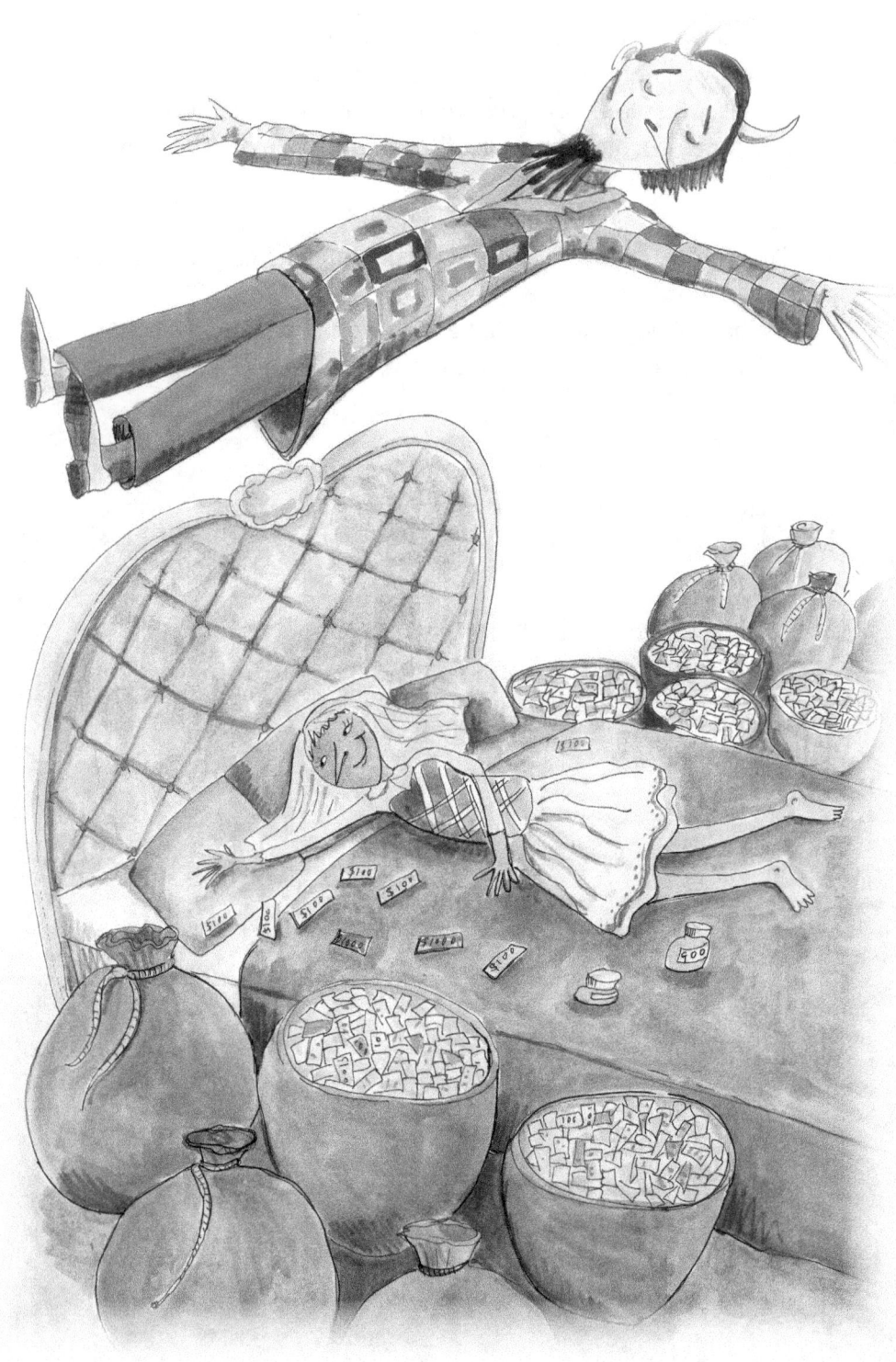

9

Not far away at Kunnikunde's castle, Mr Werner Little Werner waited outside the front entrance like an over-excited puppy for his beloved boss to appear. And, like such a puppy, he had lost some control of his bladder.

When he heard Countess Kunnikunde call out his name from the front door of the castle, he almost crawled inside to greet her, leaving a little puddle of excitement behind. Kunnikunde and the devil stood on the front step watching Werner grovelling towards them.

Just behind Werner was the impeccably attired Mr Broombridge, who was also part of the devil's official welcome party. As he made his way towards the front entrance, he stepped in Werner's little puddle of pee. Mr Broombridge's legs went out from under him, and he landed straight on his expensively trousered backside, right in the pee puddle.

'Undignified but interesting entrance,' remarked the devil. The King of Darkness was dressed exactly as he had been when he appeared at Kunnikunde's house in Snobtown the year before. He sported the same red trousers, tan shoes, black shirt, and multi-coloured jacket. Above a pale and drawn face, his hair was pitch black. Kunnikunde wore a purple dirndl skirt with a green bodice and a bottle-blonde-coloured blouse that matched her bleached long hair. Her face was a chalky salmon-pink of thickly applied makeup. Despite her extreme efforts, the ravages of age were clearly taking a terrible toll on the countess's complexion.

When Werner Little Werner finally reached his beloved Kunnikunde, he grasped her hand and started kissing it repeatedly. To Kunnikunde, it felt like a dog was slobbering all over it.

'Incompetence!' she screamed at him, wrenching her damp hand from his slimy grip. 'Total incompetence! I'm surrounded by it! Werner! ... Did you get me money? You know I can't sleep without money! Money! Money! Money!' she shouted on the edge of hysteria.

'Of course, Countess! Of course!' Werner wailed. 'There are four suitcases filled with cash next to your bed.'

Kunnikunde's mood changed instantly. She took the devil's hand and, with a sweet smile, said, 'Let me show you my humble castle. *My* castle! Mine! All mine!'

As she started to lead the devil away for his castle tour, Mr Broombridge approached them, putting on a brave face after his ignominious arrival.

'Greetings to you both,' he said. 'Forgive me for my ungainly stumble. I stepped in something slippery.'

The devil smiled civilly at Mr Broombridge, but Kunnikunde's attention wasn't on his face. Unfortunately for him, when he fell on his backside the impact jolted Mr Broombridge's wallet halfway out of his back pocket. Kunnikunde had spotted it in an instant. Suddenly Mr Broombridge was airborne and flew ten metres into the castle courtyard before landing flat on his face. Kunnikunde had tried to steal Mr Broombridge's wallet with her new, powerful extendable arm but she had been too close; all she had achieved was to catapult him to the courtyard.

This display of uncontrollable, frenzied greed was too much, even for the devil, and he started scolding Kunnikunde. 'Did we not have an agreement that for the next couple of days you would refrain from stealing anything? I have given you a right hand that's extendable for one hundred metres and made out of metal so you can hurt or kill someone who's a distance away. It's not for snatching the wallet of someone standing right next to you! Is that understood?'

'Yes, yes ... of course!' Kunnikunde wailed. 'I will only use it when you command me.'

Little Werner, who had gone ahead, now stuck his head out the front door. 'What happened to Mr Broombridge?' he asked.

'He's had a bad fall ... over in the courtyard,' Kunnikunde replied. 'You'd better call an ambulance.'

The devil took his time inspecting the castle, going from room to room, very carefully scanning every object as well as all the servants and other staff he encountered. After almost two hours, he returned to Kunnikunde's bedroom.

'The castle seems clear!' he announced. 'But there is a putrid religious smell in this place.'

'I have no idea what it could be,' Kunnikunde declared. 'Maybe some of the staff are secret God botherers, but there's no religion conducted here, I assure you! This is no church!'

The devil laughed weirdly. 'What a pity! A church is the best place for me to levitate and send out thoughts and instructions all over the universe. The smell of sinners, as all churchgoers are, is a delight and seems to infuse me with extra evil energy and enhance my demonic powers. I spend a lot of time in churches. The more God botherers in the world the better; I like it!'

That evening, Kunnikunde's servants built a roaring fire in the huge fireplace in the countess's bedroom and left for the night. And Kunnikunde, as she did every evening, sprawled out on her bed surrounded by money as she tried yet more exotic but always futile anti-ageing methods involving various kinds of fruit and vegetables and layers of thick pastes, gels and lotions.

The devil regarded her briefly with equal measures of contempt and amusement, before becoming airborne. What a picture it was! The devil, lying horizontally in mid-air, levitated across the room while Kunnikunde, lying horizontally on her bed with gooey white make-up all over her face and slices of cucumber covering her eyes, blissfully cuddled her money.

'I have to go and do my work,' the devil announced before floating into the fireplace and disappearing into the flames.

Kunnikunde's euphoric self-absorption was rudely and somewhat violently interrupted about an hour later when a fireball shot out of the fireplace and filled the room. The heat threatened to bake her facial make-up and cook the cucumber slices on her eyes. She sat bolt upright in her bed and flicked the cucumber slices off her face, sending them flying. Restored to sight, she realised to her horror that some of her money had caught fire. She let out a terrifying shriek, which seemed to snuff out all the flames, including in the fireplace itself. Suddenly the air in the room turned chilly.

Kunnikunde saw the devil standing at the foot of her bed. 'I cannot stay in this place!' he growled.

Kunnikunde hardly recognised him; she thought he looked like a werewolf.

'These irritating little good spirits,' he snarled. 'I despise them! They are the mosquitos of the spirit world! Childish little pranksters! I'm itching all over from those awful "good-thought pebbles" they put in the fireplace. They don't know it, but they're playing with fire! If they knew it was Lucifer himself they were up against, they wouldn't dare try something like that!'

He took a small mirror from the pocket of his red trousers and held it up proudly. 'This is a trap I've built that can hold up to ten of those irritating spiritual insects! There are already three of them inside. Tomorrow I'll be adding another six! Ha ha ha!'

The devil's laughter shook the whole room.

Kunnikunde barely noticed it. She was sitting up in bed still bedazzled by the fireball and could only mutter, 'You burnt some of my money! My money!'

The devil's impatience was at the breaking point. 'You want more money?' he yelled at Kunnikunde. 'Is that all you ever think about? I can give you money! Here!' He stretched out both arms and thousand-dollar notes flew from his hands at an incredible rate, showering the greedy countess with money. Pretty soon the whole room was covered in a thick layer of thousand-dollar notes.

By the time the last note floated down and settled on Kunnikunde's bottle-blonde head, the devil was gone. The greedy countess plucked the note from her hair, held it in both hands and kissed it. 'I love you!' she called after the devil. 'I want to marry you!'

It took Countess Kunnikunde hours to collect all the money, which she stuffed into empty doona covers. When she finally collapsed on her bed, exhausted, the room was packed with huge bags of money. The last sound to be heard from Kunnikunde before she fell asleep was an almost inaudible whimper: 'But, I need more.'

10

When Reverend Semmelmeier opened the side door of his church with his big key and stepped inside, he was confronted by a strange and disturbing sight. There in front of the altar was a man floating horizontally about a metre off the polished timber floor, seemingly in a deep trance.

The reverend's first instinct was to flee, but as he started for the door, he stopped and gathered himself. *This is MY church!* he told himself. *MY domain! The Almighty God is here and will protect me.* 'You, there!' he called, cautiously advancing towards the floating figure. 'What kind of trick is this? Who are you? Under what authority have you entered a locked church?'

The devil gradually came out of his trance, his body slowly tilting vertically until his feet were firmly on the floor. His eyes glowed red as they scanned the reverend's entire body.

If Reverend Semmelmeier had been alarmed at the man's levitation, his glowing red eyes were positively terrifying. 'Who ... who are you?' he gasped, ready to flee once again.

'I'm a magician,' the devil said affably.

The reverend visibly relaxed, expelling a big breath of air. 'Ahh, I see.'

'I have an avid interest in churches,' the devil continued. 'I'm something of an expert.'

'Well, as you can see,' the reverend said with a sweeping gesture of his hand, 'this is a very beautiful church.'

'Are you the local priest?' the devil asked.

'No, I'm the local reverend, Mr Semmelmeier.'

The two chatted amiably for a time, the devil showing a particular interest in the reverend's upcoming routine for the next few days.

The revered was happy to oblige him with details. 'The only important event coming up soon is the holy meal I will be blessing in two days, which is to be served at Count Johann von Ritter's sixtieth birthday party. Why don't you come along as part of my flock and join in the celebrations?'

'I will! I certainly will!' the devil responded enthusiastically. At that, he walked straight into Reverend Semmelmeier's body to possess it. There was a brief struggle as the poor reverend's body jerked up and down several times, but within seconds it calmed down. The devil had successfully taken over Reverend Semmelmeier's body.

'A corpulent, vertically challenged body,' the devil remarked to himself out loud. 'But it will do the job.'

11

After a long, restful sleep dreaming about money, Kunnikunde awoke refreshed and ready to rain chaos and terror on the citizens of Stone and one ten-year-old boy and his family in particular.

She shrieked when she saw Reverend Semmelmeier standing at the foot of her bed. 'Reverend! Get out of my bedroom! What do you think you're doing?'

'Saving you from the devil,' the reverend's body replied.

'I don't need to be saved from that loser!' Kunnikunde shouted, angrily. 'I'm not afraid of anyone—not even Lucifer himself. If I should marry him, I'll gradually force him to pass on all his powers to me so that I can take over as the Queen of Darkness! And then, my chubby little reverend, I will own all the money in the universe!'

At that thought, Kunnikunde's face beamed with the happiest smile, but within seconds it was distorted with hate and disgust. 'Get out of my castle!' she shrieked at the reverend. *'Raus! Raus!* Out! Out!'

'You are fascinating me, Kunnikunde,' the devil reverend said calmly. Then his eyes glowed red and his tone became suddenly sinister. 'What an interesting confession!' he snarled.

Kunnikunde immediately realised her terrible mistake and tried to bluff her way out of it. 'I knew it was you,' she muttered unconvincingly. 'I just played along with your silly game.'

'I don't play games, Kunnikunde!' the devil reverend growled, furious. He sniffed the air like a wild predator. 'I can smell those vile insect spirits! We have work to do! We must go into town now!'

Kunnikunde's protest was immediate and loud. 'No way!' she shouted. 'The people of Stone will recognise me instantly!'

'Not in this disguise,' the devil reverend retorted with an evil smile. He waved his hand in Kunnikunde's direction and she turned into a very plain, chubby woman with mean piggy eyes who looked like she enjoyed her food and wine rather too much and wasn't fussy about her appearance.

Kunnikunde stood in front of one of the several mirrors in her bedroom. 'AAAAAARRRGH!' she screeched. 'I look horrible! I look like a piggy, common housewife! I'm an aristocrat ... a career woman! I will not go out like this. Never!'

'OK, you're right,' the devil reverend said. 'Your outfit is missing an essential accessory.' With that, he flicked his hand once and a big ugly, tattered handbag appeared hanging over Piggy Kunnikunde's right shoulder.

'Put your right hand in the bag,' the devil reverend commanded. 'It will hide your iron fist.'

Before Piggy Kunnikunde could say anything else he touched her on her hand and they both vanished, reappearing a second later in the middle of the Stone township.

12

Not far from where Lucifer and Kunnikunde materialised, the painter, Fritz, knocked at Police Chief Wurstling's door. 'I'm here to paint your garage door,' he called out.

'About time!' he heard Wurstling's voice thunder behind the door. 'You were supposed to be here two weeks ago!'

The door opened to reveal Commander Wurstling in his pyjamas with a fat sausage roll in his hand. 'You tradesmen—always late! The garage is this way,' he growled, brushing past Fritz.

'It won't take any time at all,' the painter said.

When they reached the garage, Wurstling started explaining what he wanted done and that he demanded the highest quality job.

As Fritz shuffled impatiently, listening to Wurstling's ranting, he unintentionally touched the garage door ever so slightly with his brand-new brush that the magic pencil had made especially for him. At once, a mighty blue flash engulfed the garage and the entire house along with it.

Commander Wurstling was so startled he dropped his sausage roll. He bent down and picked it up, but he immediately dropped it again in astonishment. He saw that not only did the garage look brand new, but his whole house looked like it had been built yesterday. All the moss on the roof was gone and the copper gutters and downpipes now sparkled in the sun. What Wurstling couldn't yet see, of course, was that the same thing had happened inside his house.

Fritz, equally dumbfounded, was stunned into silence.

After about thirty seconds, Wurstling started to compose himself. 'Fritz, you are an idiot! How can you quote an hourly rate when you have such talent and work so quickly? You'll make nothing. You should quote on a finished job.'

Fritz had begun to recover too and, at last, managed to say something. 'Magic! Magic!' he cried, wide-eyed, holding his paintbrush up in front of him. 'Magic brush! I have a magic brush!'

Only such severe shock could have caused Commander Wurstling to forget that his sausage roll was still on the ground. Now recovered, he remembered it. He bent down to retrieve it, but he was a second too late. The neighbour's rottweiler dog saw its chance and took it, snatching the sausage roll just before Wurstling's fingers could grasp it. The commander yelled out a colourful word as he watched the dog run next door with his sausage roll in its mouth.

Forgetting the extraordinary transformation of his house, he ran inside. He re-emerged thirty seconds later, still in his pyjamas, holding a notepad and pencil in one hand and jamming his police hat on his head with the other. In this comical uniform, he stormed over to his neighbour's house to arrest the sausage-roll-thieving rottweiler.

Painter Fritz was still standing entranced with his magic brush when he heard a voice right behind him. He turned to see the beaming face of Devil Reverend Semmelmeier.

'What a magnificent paintbrush,' he said cheerily. 'May I have a look at it?'

What happened next took no longer than the blink of an eye, but to the devil reverend, it looked like slow motion. He grabbed Fritz's brush with one hand, pulled out his mirror with the other and shoved the brush deep into the mirror, his entire arm disappearing into it too. Then, with a quick yank, he pulled the brush back out of the mirror, which flashed a bright blue. He returned the mirror to his pocket and put the brush back into Fritz's hand. It had all happened too fast for Fritz's eyes and brain to process it.

Fritz put his brush in his bag and looked around for Mr Semmelmeier to resume their conversation, but the devil reverend was gone.

I must be hallucinating, Fritz thought as he wandered off towards his home.

Next door, Commander Wurstling confronted his neighbour.

'Bit early for a drink, isn't it, Commander?' the neighbour remarked. 'You're not sleepwalking, are you?'

'Hugo!' Wurstling barked, 'I'm here on official police business. I'm not here to socialise!'

'What's happened?' Hugo asked, concerned. 'We haven't done anything wrong. It must be a misunderstanding.'

'It's about your criminal, thieving dog!' Wurstling explained angrily. 'He stole police property!'

'Oh no!' Hugo cried. 'Not a pistol or a baton, I hope?'

'No! It was a sausage roll!' Wurstling shouted.

His relieved neighbour couldn't suppress a chuckle.

'This is no laughing matter, Hugo!' Wurstling said. 'This is serious!'

'Where was this stolen object, exactly?' Hugo asked. 'Did my dog rip it out of your hand?'

'Not quite. It was on the ground between my feet. I was about to pick it up.'

'Wurstling! Wurstling!' Hugo exclaimed, shaking his head. 'You have no idea about animal instincts and behaviour. Anything on the ground—especially food—a dog assumes is its property if it finds it first. The ground is a dog's domain. For them, possession is ten-tenths of the law, not nine.'

'I will still have to interview the suspect,' Wurstling declared.

'Not a good idea at this particular time of the day. Sniper—that's his name—is quite frisky in the mornings and might accidentally give you a good bite.'

Wurstling was impatient to get out through the sliding glass doors to the back garden where he could see the dog lying beside its kennel.

'Sniper is trained to be a guard dog, as you know,' Hugo said, trying to stop Wurstling from storming outside.

'Stand aside, Hugo,' Wurstling commanded. 'I'm sure your dog will respect the authority of a Teutonian police officer.' He slid open the door and stepped into the garden. 'You stay out of it, Hugo.'

13

Sniper looked more like a bear than a dog. The instant he saw the commander in the garden he rushed over to him. Rather than bite the intruder, as Hugo fully expected he might, the huge rottweiler jumped up onto Wurstling and began licking his face exuberantly, almost knocking him off his feet in the process.

'Down! Down! You dumb dog!' the commander shouted, pushing Sniper down. 'Sit!' he commanded.

To Hugo's total disbelief, as he watched from the other side of the sliding glass door, Sniper sat. He hung his head in shame while Wurstling lectured him with a wagging finger.

Hugo was shaking his head in amazement, expecting his dog to be ripping into the commander's brightly striped pyjamas or chewing on his police hat.

Neither man knew that the previous year the magic pencil had passed on a permanent animal love spell to the commander while he was trying to protect Andy from the circus lions. It was the same spell that Sassy was accidentally given. Just as with Sassy, every animal loved Commander Wurstling.

A couple of minutes into his berating of Sniper, it was clear Wurstling's heart was melting at the sight of the guilty-looking dog. Despite his stern appearance and authoritarian manner, under the shell, Wurstling was a big softie. He was the kind of policeman who never hesitated to help people, even if his own life was on the line. That's why the citizens of Stone loved and respected him.

When Wurstling knelt on one knee to pet Sniper, the huge dog went berserk with love, pushing the police chief over and licking him profusely. By the time Wurstling freed himself, he looked frazzled, and his normally well-groomed hair was all over the place.

Back inside behind the safety of the sliding door, Wurstling shook his head at Hugo and said, 'Your dog is exceptionally friendly, very strong and heavy and obviously well-fed. The last thing he needed was to eat my sausage roll!'

Meanwhile, just around the corner, big Hermann the plumber was trying to repair the downpipes on old Mrs Rottweiler's house. Habitually for Hermann, his first approach to repairing anything was to use force. In most circumstances, this only served to make the repair job even bigger. But not today! When Hermann found he couldn't bend the pipe he was working on, despite using all his considerable strength, he grabbed his brand-new hammer and gave the pipe a mighty whack. Thor the God of Thunder himself couldn't have delivered a more spectacular blow. The entire house lit up with a dazzling blue flash as if it had been hit by a blue lightning bolt. Hermann was momentarily blinded. When Mrs Rottweiler appeared at the front door and spoke to him, he could hear her voice but couldn't see her.

'Are you still alive, Hermann?' she cried out. 'A lightning strike has hit the house, turning everything brand new!'

Hermann was too dazed to speak and just nodded his head. This head movement was enough to answer Mrs Rottweiler's question to her satisfaction. Before she went back inside the house, she called to Hermann, 'Tell Reverend Semmelmeier standing behind you that I don't need to see him yet.' With that, Hermann heard her close the front door.

Hermann's vision had cleared just enough for him to recognise the reverend, who was now standing in front of him. He didn't know the rather chubby woman with him.

'That's a magnificent hammer,' the devil reverend said, smiling. 'May I see it?'

Then, with Hermann's hammer, the devil did exactly as he had done earlier with Fritz's paintbrush. Before Hermann knew anything had happened, the devil reverend handed the hammer back to him.

Hermann watched him wander off with his chubby female companion.

Back at the castle, Piggy Kunnikunde started pleading with the devil reverend to change her back to her usual self, except she wanted him to make her thirty years younger. He just laughed and began scolding her unmercifully, giving her a proper dressing down.

'This has been your problem right from the beginning!' he yelled. 'Uncontrollable, excessive vanity and greed. Your strategic thinking is dysfunctional! Your ability to focus is like that of a toddler! For once in your life, follow my orders! Do you want victory ... or don't you?'

'Of course, I do,' muttered a subdued Kunnikunde.

'In that case, we follow my quite simple strategy! First, we disarm our enemies and then—ONLY THEN—we kill them! Is that understood?'

'Yes! Yes!' whined Piggy Kunnikunde.

The devil reverend left her moaning to herself and went back up onto the roof of the big tower. He began scanning the town and its surrounding area for any sign of blue flashes or other spiritual phenomena.

He could see the von Ritter house from his vantage point but didn't detect any spiritual activity thanks to the scanning-shield outfits Michaela had built for herself and Andy.

Despite her confidence in their outfits' effectiveness against the devil's powers, Michaela was uncharacteristically anxious, even nervous. She walked slowly around the large dining room in circles, her head cocked to one side as if she were intently listening for sounds of some kind. Suddenly she stopped dead in her tracks, looked straight at Andy and began rattling off instructions to him. He had heard them before, but she wanted to make sure he'd remembered them. 'This is the sign I'll make to you when the devil is present.' She formed her two index fingers into a cross. At that point, we have no other communication—with our voices nor our thoughts. You are to stand still and focus on relaxing your jaw as this will greatly reduce your capacity to think—and hopefully empty your mind of any thoughts whatsoever. That way the devil won't be able to read your thoughts. You are to carry the replica magic pencil I gave you in your front pocket at all times and ensure part of it is clearly visible to the devil.'

Michaela's sudden intensity and anxious tone made Andy extremely nervous, even frightened. 'When's he coming? When?'

'A very short time after we've finished building the barn for your father's birthday celebrations,' Michaela answered, her usual calm tone returning, much to Andy's relief. 'My two spirit friends from Fritz's paintbrush and Hermann's hammer are already on their mission,' she added.

'How do you know?' Andy asked, frowning.

'Their signals have stopped. That's what I was listening for earlier. They are both in the devil's trap.'

'What?' Andy exclaimed. 'That's not good ... is it?'

'It's part of the plan,' Michaela answered. 'Each of them is strong enough to destroy the trap and escape.'

'Why haven't they escaped then?'

'It's not time yet. We have a plan, and we stick to it as a team. They know exactly when to escape.' Remember; working alone, however great you may be as an individual, rarely leads to success. You need teamwork! The positive spirit and energy of a team definitely lead to success!'

'But we are alone in the house. It's just the two of us, not the whole team! Mum's out shopping and Dad won't be back until tomorrow.'

'That was the idea exactly, Andy,' Michaela said. 'Kunnikunde wants to kill you all at the same time, and for her to do that you have to all be together. And that will be tomorrow night at Johann's birthday party. That will be your evil aunt's first opportunity to have her hired assassins do her dirty work for her.'

14

To Andy, it sounded as if Michaela was actually looking forward to the assassination attempt! He watched her stride to the front door and somehow produce the building plans for the big barn she had drawn up a few days earlier, which she had bound into a thick document. Andy was surprised at how many pages there were. What happened next eliminated any negative thoughts he had.

Michaela laid the plans document on the dining table, took the replica pencil from Andy's pocket, removed its silver cover and placed the pencil on top of the document. The pencil now took on a life of its own. With incredible speed, it flicked through page after page of the plans as if it were memorising the details of the building's construction. Then suddenly it disappeared. Shortly after, a huge blue flash filled the sky above the wide lawn area outside where the big barn would be erected for Johann's birthday party. Less than a second later, the pencil was back in Andy's front pocket.

Michaela suddenly barked an order at Andy. 'No more communication, Andy!'

She crossed her index fingers, signalling to Andy that the devil was present. She then rushed into the living room and flopped into a chair, pretending to be reading a book. Andy stood gaping after her, not sure what to do next. A loud knock on the back door snapped him to attention. Before he could move to answer it, he found himself face-to-face with Reverend Semmelmeier and a very chubby, piggish-looking woman with fierce eyes. They were perhaps the only recognisable feature of his Aunt Kunnikunde's disguise, but Andy missed it.

Without a word, Piggy Kunnikunde went straight into the dining room while the devil reverend spoke to Andy. 'What a beautiful writing instrument you have in your pocket, little boy.'

At that moment, Andy thought he saw a faint blue flash in the reverend's face. But he didn't see what happened next. It was all over in the blink of an eye; the devil did his usual thing. With supersonic speed, he removed the pencil from Andy's pocket, plunged it deep into his mirror, pulled it out and replaced it in Andy's pocket. Andy was none the wiser.

Even as he continued a one-way conversation with Andy, the devil reverend was flicking his eyes around the room scanning everything in sight.

Faithfully following Michaela's instructions, Andy stood motionless, so glassy-eyed and slack-jawed that he started to dribble. He looked like the dumbest boy in Stone.

The devil reverend scanned Andy all over but wasn't surprised he found no spirit activity in such a stupid-looking boy. He excused himself and went over to Michaela who politely put down her book and looked up at him.

'Hello, little girl,' the devil reverend said, pleasantly enough. 'What's your name?'

'I'm Michaela.'

'What are you doing here?'

'I'm a friend of Andy's cousins, Gracie and Belle,' Michaela answered, smiling sweetly. 'My parents are away on a trip, and I'm staying here for a few days.'

The devil reverend nodded and then walked through to the dining room, just in time to witness the cause of a blood-curdling scream that could have been heard all over Stone.

Even in her new form, Kunnikunde couldn't help being greedy. With all the valuables and silverware in the house locked up and out of her reach, she had homed in on two magnificent silver goblets perched on top of the dining room cabinet. Looking at them, Kunnikunde had no concept whatsoever of just how solid and heavy they were. One goblet was right at the edge so she decided that if she nudged it with her iron fist it would topple over, and she could catch it in her big bag.

The idea wasn't bad, but the execution was a total disaster. Underestimating the power of her iron fist, she struck the heavy goblet far too hard, turning it into a bone-crunching missile that flew off the cabinet and crash-landed on her left foot. Kunnikunde actually heard the bones crunching just before the sound was obliterated by her blood-curdling scream of pain.

The devil reverend grabbed Kunnikunde under the arms as she started to fall to the floor and then physically manhandled her from the dining room and out the front door.

Andy was so focused on his slack-jawed stupid boy pose that he seemed to have sent himself into some kind of self-hypnotic trance.

'Snap out of it, silly boy!' Michaela commanded, giving him a slight slap.

It worked. 'That was scary!' Andy cried. I didn't know that Reverend Semmelmeier was the devil! Living all the time right here in Stone ... running the church! Unbelievable!'

'The devil just took over the reverend's body temporarily, you idiot,' Michaela said, rolling her eyes.

'Are you sure?' Andy asked, wide-eyed.

'Positive!' Michaela retorted. 'As if Lucifer would confine himself to a little church in Stone when he has the whole cosmos to choose from! Ridiculous!'

Andy realised just how ridiculous his reaction had been and looked suitably embarrassed. 'Um ... yeah ... true,' he mumbled.

'By the way,' Michaela said, 'did you notice? The devil always arrives through the back door and leaves through the front door.'

'Yes!' Andy gasped. 'I've never seen the reverend use our back door. You're right!'

'Of course, I'm right, you garlic brain!' Michaela snapped, standing with her hands on her hips.

Another rather willing conversation ensued between them when Andy declared that he didn't think the devil reverend touched the pencil in his pocket. 'It didn't move. I was watching it closely.'

'He touched it, all right,' Michaela said. 'He also put it into his mirror trap, took it out again and placed it back in your pocket—all in a thousandth of a second.

'No way!' Andy yelled. 'Impossible!'

'You're impossible!' Michaela yelled back at him. 'Anyway, as far as I'm concerned the first part of my mission is complete!'

Andy still looked like he wanted to argue, but Michaela started towards the front door. 'There is still much work to do before the mission is completely finished. Let's go and look at the big barn. It should be built by now.'

With Andy still muttering grumpily to himself and Michaela doing her best to ignore him, they headed for the wide lawn area next to the driveway.

15

'Change me back to my old self!' Kunnikunde pleaded with the devil between screams of pain as she writhed around on her giant-sized bed. 'Please! Please! I can't stand this pain.'

'Cannot and will not do!' growled the devil. 'It was your own stupid, greedy fault!' He snapped his fingers and a large bottle of pills appeared on one of Kunnikunde's bedside tables.

'Take some of those painkillers,' the devil snarled, 'but not too many or they'll kill *you* along with the pain.'

His expression suggested that he thought that wouldn't be such a bad thing.

Kunnikunde gulped down several of the pills and immediately felt the pain start to ease. She began to relax.

The devil reverend was far from relaxed. He was so angry with Kunnikunde that his foul mood turned him into a hideous werewolf version of Mr Semmelmeier.

It was at this very untimely moment that Mr Werner Little Werner chose to enter the room and find out what all the screaming was about. When the werewolf devil reverend looked at him and howled savagely, Werner wet himself again. He fell to his knees in his own puddle and then crawled over to the devil, who had resumed the normal visage of Reverend Semmelmeier. Werner grabbed the devil reverend's hand and started kissing it profusely.

'Master! Master! I want to serve you!' he wailed. 'The countess means nothing to me! Please! Please!'

'Of course, you can, Werner,' the devil reverend said. 'You can be my second set of eyes.'

Little Werner was beside himself with excitement. 'Thank you! Thank you, master!' he cried. He suddenly realised there was another person in the bedroom. 'What is that ugly dumpling doing on the countess's bed?'

'That is your former boss, whom you have just denounced,' the devil reverend replied with a smirk.

Werner didn't get a chance to respond because, yet again, Kunnikunde couldn't help herself. With a banshee screech, she launched her iron fist at Werner's head. She would have removed Werner's head from his shoulders if the devil reverend hadn't caught her fist right in front of Werner's horrified face.

The devil reverend finally lost his temper and went ballistic. 'Will you never learn?' he screamed at Kunnikunde, involuntarily turning into the werewolf version of the reverend again. From Kunnikunde's viewpoint, he looked hideous and terrifying. 'Can you not listen? Can you not follow the simplest strategy? Must you always lose control like an emotional child? This could be your last chance to rid yourself of the family you hate so much!'

He was so angry he clicked his fingers again and the bottle of painkillers exploded into a cloud of dust. Kunnikunde's pain instantly returned.

'AAAAAARRRRRGGGHHH!' she screeched. 'Please! Please! Make it stop!'

'Will not do!' the devil reverend snarled with a malicious grin. 'It's self-inflicted! You deserve every bit of it. I enjoy seeing people in pain! I love pain and misery! I'm even tempted to increase your pain to teach you a lesson. However, I still have a use for you, so I'll have Werner drive you to the hospital.'

Now aware that the ugly dumpling, as he had called her, was his beloved Countess Kunnikunde, Werner looked profoundly embarrassed and deeply repentant as he moved across to help Kunnikunde from the bed.

'Countess, Countess,' he grovelled, 'how could I have possibly known it was you?'

Kunnikunde looked right through him with her fierce piggy eyes and refused to respond. Nothing Werner could possibly say or do was going to change the fact she had heard him denounce her in favour of the devil.

'Werner!' the devil reverend barked at him. 'Under no circumstances are you to introduce Miss Chubby Piggy here as the countess. Her true identity must be kept hidden at all costs!'

'Yes, master!' Werner squeaked, bowing. He could feel Kunnikunde's eyes shooting bullets into the back of his grovelling head, but he forced himself not to look at her.

When they got to the hospital, Werner arranged for some crutches for Kunnikunde and helped her into the emergency reception where several other patients were waiting for treatment. From habit, he almost announced the arrival of Countess Kunnikunde Ritter von Krumm. Only at the last second did he manage to stop himself. Instead, he overcompensated and called out loudly, 'This hideous chubby woman needs some help with her fat broken foot.'

'Chauvinist pig!' were the last words Little Werner heard before Lady Heger-Steel's fearsome hand made contact with his face, knocking him unconscious to the floor.

'Come with me, my beautiful lady,' Lady Heger-Steel said as she guided chubby Kunnikunde towards the nurses' station. Piggy Kunnikunde received preferred treatment because the nurses felt sorry for her being stuck with such a horrible little man.

They x-rayed her foot and gave have her painkilling injections. *If they knew who I really was,* Piggy Kunnikunde thought, *the injections would be lethal!* They also gave her enough analgesics to last a month. Eventually, she was shown to a seat to wait for a medical moon boot, which would allow her to walk while the broken bones in her foot healed.

It turned out that Lady Heger-Steel wasn't at the hospital because she needed medical assistance. Rather, she was waiting for a little boy who had fallen off a porch at school while skylarking and broken his arm.

Piggy Kunnikunde, to her great surprise, felt quite happy and relaxed with the pain gone and waited patiently for her medical moon boot.

16

In the meantime, Werner had regained consciousness and with the begrudging assistance of a nurse was now sitting down holding an ice pack to one side of his face. He was only vaguely aware of his assailant, Lady Heger-Steel, dragging the little boy with the broken arm out of the waiting room by his left ear, explaining in no uncertain terms, 'If you fall off the porch again acting like an idiot, I will give you a belting all the way to the hospital—with a run-up!'

As was his unfortunate habit, Mr Broombridge's appearance was hopelessly ill-timed once again. After treatment for his injuries at the hand of Kunnikunde in the castle courtyard, he was hobbling through the reception area when Piggy Kunnikunde spotted him.

'Mr Broombridge!' she exclaimed. 'How are you?'

Mr Broombridge turned around and almost recoiled with disgust. 'I'm the boss of the Ritter von Krumm company. I don't converse with overweight, lowly riff-raff workers!' In his wildest dreams, he could never have imagined this repugnant piggy commoner was Countess Kunnikunde.

As he turned to walk away, he saw the one woman on the planet he had no wish to see, ever again. *It's that crazed Heger-Steel monster!*

A second woman he later wished he might never see again, called out to him. 'Mr Broombridge,' the disguised Piggy Kunnikunde asked politely, 'What about Countess Kunnikunde? Isn't she the boss? Does she not run the Ritter von Krumm company?'

'Ha!' answered the now distracted Broombridge. 'That crazy dumb woman couldn't run a bath! I have her under full control! She has no say whatsoever! She does exactly what I tell her!' As he spoke, he still kept a wary eye on Lady Heger-Steel.

Broombridge's outrageous remarks were too much for Kunnikunde. She instantly wielded her iron fist with devastating effect. It hit poor Mr Broombridge so hard that he was immediately airborne. The impact broke one of his crutches, but he held the other one out straight, like a lance, as he flew across the reception area. What finally brought him to an abrupt halt was the very ample bulk of Lady Heger-Steel. She crashed to the ground, with Mr Broombridge on top of her. He desperately looked around for his crutch so he could get back on his feet. To his horror, he saw it firmly embedded in the Heger-Steel monster's monstrous bottom.

When he tried to extract it, all hell broke loose! For the other patients in the reception area, the violence inflicted on Mr Broombridge by Lady Heger-Steel was too brutal to watch and they covered their eyes. Regrettably, they couldn't cover their ears at the same time, and they heard the word 'PERVERT!' screamed out over and over again.

Sometime later, peace and calm were restored to the hospital reception when Lady Heger-Steel departed the premises and Mr Broombridge was carried to the emergency room. He was soon in a hospital bed covered in bandages yet again. A nurse came in and told him he should be ashamed of himself for touching up married women and that he should cease and desist forthwith. It was at this point Mr Broombridge broke down and sobbed. 'She even bit my legs!'

In the meantime, Piggy Kunnikunde's moon boot had been fitted, and she hobbled out accompanied by Little Werner still clutching the ice pack to his black and blue face. Kunnikunde looked a lot happier with herself, although she hadn't yet stood in front of a full-length mirror to see how ridiculous the big moon boot looked on her.

Kunnikunde was no longer talking to Little Werner after he had vowed to serve the devil rather than her. Once back at the castle, she refused to have anything to do with him. *I seem to be the only person in this world who is loyal to me and defends my interests*, she lamented to herself. *I cannot trust anyone!*

When the devil reverend came down from the big tower roof, he looked pleased with himself, but he scanned the room again just to be sure no more good spirits had returned.

'I can understand your difficulties with these nasty little blue flashing insect spirits!' the devil reverend said. 'Especially the last one that inhabited the boy's pencil—it had a lot of energy and put up quite a fight when I caught it!'

'I still think it is my nephew, Andy!' Kunnikunde exclaimed. 'He definitely has supernatural powers! I saw it with my own eyes!'

'Rubbish, Kunnikunde!' the devil reverend shouted. 'You're losing your grip—you're imagining things! I myself stood right in front of that boy and scanned him three times. There was nothing! And I detected little or no brain waves—which means he's also very dumb! Ha ha ha!'

'I think you are wrong—very wrong!' Kunnikunde yelled at the devil. 'I'm telling you—it's Andy! He can change his appearance. He seems to be able to teleport himself. And he can also tame wild animals! It's that boy you should be after!'

The devil began to lose his temper and as usual, when he got very angry, his form started switching back and forth between his temporary human form and his actual hideous werewolf-like self.

'What would you know about what you call "supernatural"?' he snarled. 'These incompetent minor spirits can easily fool you— but not me. I'm the King of Darkness! I can also make myself undetectable to them. They obviously did not expect me, Lucifer, to come to this godforsaken place! They were unprepared and therefore carelessly assumed they were only up against mere demons and minor devils. Ha ha ha!'

'But I've seen Andy's powers with my own eyes!' Kunnikunde wailed.

'The strong spirit I trapped from the boy's pencil could easily have taken over his body and performed all those tricks you saw. Those spirits are also specially trained in building "good-thought bombs," which you have been a victim of. And they are very annoying to me!'

Kunnikunde ceased her protesting and seemed to give up, but she still did not look completely convinced the devil was right.

Werner Little Werner, who had come in and begun grovelling to the devil reverend, had no such doubts. 'You are so right, master!' he squeaked.

If looks could kill, Werner would have instantly collapsed to the floor stone dead from the vicious glare Kunnikunde gave him. Instead, the little weasel just heard her mumble, 'I trust no one.'

Ignoring Werner and his crawling, the devil reverend set about detailing his plans for the second part of the mission to kill Johann and his family.

'It will be a delightful event!' Lucifer declared, laughing uproariously. 'Having caught all their protective spirits, the family is now defenceless! And my inspired disguise as the local reverend is perfect for turning ordinary people into murderous assassins,' he gloated.

It took him almost half an hour to explain his detailed and diabolical plan to Werner and Kunnikunde. The instant he finished, Werner applauded wildly. 'Bravo, master!' he cried. 'Brilliant! Brilliant!'

Kunnikunde wasn't nearly as enthusiastic. 'Why go to all this complicated effort just to kill three defenceless people?' she asked, reasonably enough. 'Let's just go over to my brother-in-law's house right now, kill Anna and Andy and the little girl if she's there—and then wait for Johann to return and kill him the moment he walks in the front door?' She brushed her hands together several times as if to say, *There! Simple! Job done!*

The devil could hardly believe his ears that someone would dare question his plans—and come up with an alternative plan! He exploded. 'How can you be so careless and stupid?' he screeched at Kunnikunde. 'Killing is an art—not just a murderous act where the pleasure is all over in an instant! The satisfaction must be extended and drawn out to truly appreciate the joys of killing! That's why it's an art! The art of getting innocent people convicted for a murder they did not commit! The art of relishing the sorrow of the community! And, last but not least, the art of not being caught!' He paused, assuming he had irrefutably made his point.

'Too self-indulgent. Too complicated,' Kunnikunde retorted. 'My plan is much—'

The devil was incandescent with rage and instantly morphed into his hideous werewolf-like self. 'Your idiotic plan,' he howled, 'is doomed to fail! Johann's place will be full of workers and servants setting up for the big party tomorrow, and they'll probably be working through the night. And I'm sure that buffoon police chief, Wurstling, will already have a security detachment on-site; this is Count Johann and his family we're talking about here, the most important and popular family in Stone! Wurstling won't be taking any chances with their safety!'

The devil had finally worn Kunnikunde down; she had run out of arguments. Lucifer threw his hands in the air with relief. He then turned to Werner and gave him a big bundle of money.

'Pick up Countess Kunnikunde here tomorrow afternoon at five thirty sharp. Then collect me at the church at six o'clock and drive us to Johann's birthday celebration.' He turned to Kunnikunde who was staring angrily at the bundle of money Werner was clutching in his hand.

'To maximise the pleasure, the killing of your hated family will happen at the most festive moment! Ha ha ha! Please show some patience, Kunnikunde!'

Kunnikunde wasn't listening and couldn't take her eyes off the money in Werner's hand. 'Why did you give this little weasel money?' she shrieked. 'My money! It should be mine!'

'It was my money!' the devil howled. 'But just to shut you up and keep you distracted until tomorrow afternoon … here!'

He opened his hands and a whirlwind of money streamed out, quickly filling the room with a thick layer of thousand-dollar notes.

When Kunnikunde opened her mouth to say she wanted even more, the devil shot a big bundle of notes into the gaping hole and then vanished.

17

Michaela was no less meticulous about preparing for her plan than the devil was for his. She took hours inspecting the venue specially built for the big birthday party before she was finally satisfied.

And what a venue it was! Built of stone and timber, with large black supporting beams, the structure looked more like an exhibition hall than a big simple shed. It included a fully furnished upstairs apartment with a balcony. The hall itself was equipped with benches and tables and chairs that could seat at least three thousand people. Most impressive of all was the highly polished timber dance floor adjoining a perfectly designed stage for the band, with all the sound equipment built in.

Andy couldn't believe what he was seeing. He was standing wide-eyed with amazement when he heard a very familiar voice call out. 'The cleaners have done a wonderful job rejuvenating our old hall!' Anna exclaimed.

Her remark confused Andy totally. *What old hall?* he thought. He was about to set his mother right about the brand-new venue when Michaela interrupted his thoughts.

'Pssst!' he heard her say. He looked around to see Michaela waving at him from the other side of the hall. 'Don't say anymore!' she ordered telepathically. 'Come over here.'

Andy did as he was told. 'What's Mum talking about?' he asked as soon as he reached her.

'Once I'd finished building this structure,' Michaela said, 'I sent out a false memory signal to everyone within a fifty-mile radius, making them think there had always been an old hall on this spot.'

'Why?' Andy asked impulsively, not really thinking it through.

Michaela rolled her eyes. 'Because, banana brain, most people would realise there had never been a huge building here—so how could it suddenly appear? And when your father saw it, he would totally freak out; he would know a building like this would take at least a year to build, not one day.'

'But Dad's more than fifty miles away—he won't get your signal!'

'I'll send him a separate one as soon as he's back in Stone before he gets to the house.'

'We'll have to wait for him at the station,' Andy said. 'I know which train he'll be on.'

'Good. Go and wait for him at the station, but don't let him see you. As soon as he gets off the train, immediately teleport yourself back here. Then I'll send him the signal.'

'OK, great!' Andy said.

'Giving everyone a false memory about the building is also helpful in another way,' Michaela explained. 'If everyone thinks it's always been here, then so will the devil if he scans their thoughts, which he probably will. He's suspicious of everything.'

'But if he scans it, he'll know it's spirit-built!' Andy exclaimed.

'No, he won't. I've deliberately built in some human error. He'll think that spirit builders wouldn't make mistakes. And if he thinks the building's been here for many years, he'll be relaxed enough for me to lure him into the trap I've made for him.'

Michaela then explained to Andy various plans she had for getting the devil to walk into her trap which she had set for him at the back door.

'He always enters a building through the back door,' Andy said, looking pleased with himself.

'Exactly, Andy!' Michaela said, impressed. 'You remembered. You do listen sometimes, after all!'

'I'm not always a banana brain,' he retorted with a laugh.

'Thankfully not!' Michaela responded. 'Here's something else to remember: this structure has many spiritual features. Some you might experience tonight and tomorrow at the party, others possibly during another journey, or perhaps never. Who knows? But make sure you remember any you do notice ... and keep your wits about you whenever you're in this building.'

18

The evil countess was now the only person in Stone who knew the building was brand new because Michaela's false memory signal didn't work on her due to her demonic powers. This was cause for concern for Michaela and she had to address it before Kunnikunde arrived for the party.

The large car park next to the building was also an area that Michaela inspected very carefully. Her main focus was whether or not one could see inside the building from the car park if its window shutters were open. She had opened them all to check and was very happy with the view she had of the building's interior. At that moment, she could see people bustling about inside, busily setting up for the following day's festivities.

Meanwhile, five hundred kilometres north of Stone, a weird-looking flying machine took off in dramatic circumstances. Dr Folterknecht's escape from the insane asylum was well planned. During his time there he had become a model inmate. As the former boss of the Teutonian Secret Police, he was allowed to work for three days a week at their head office. He was assigned the task of designing and constructing the tranquilliser darts the secret police planned to use to control anti-government demonstrations.

Folterknecht also had a special interest in a large manned drone that had a range of one thousand kilometres. He helped to develop a poisonous dart gun for the drone that could take out hundreds of people in less than a minute. Not only that but the propellers of this deadly drone could be retracted, turning it into a kind of armoured car. With his usual cunning, Folterknecht befriended the pilots who taught him how to handle this unique machine.

First thing this morning, Folterknecht had loaded the drone's guns with hundreds of darts, sat himself in the pilot's seat and started the engines.

'Achtung! Achtung! Stop!' a security guard cried out. Instantly about thirty secret police officers rushed towards Folterknecht. He lifted off, hovered low to the ground for several seconds and took out every police officer with his dart gun, more accurately described as a dart machine gun. As he zoomed the drone out of the hangar, he shot several guards on the security wall. He then angled the craft almost vertically and flew straight up high into the sky. From inside the drone, he heard the blaring sirens fade into silence below him.

Folterknecht then levelled out and rubbed his hands together with immense satisfaction. Next, he set the craft's flight path with the voice-controlled GPS satnav and leaned back in his seat feeling extremely pleased with himself. He again rubbed his hands together vigorously with excitement and expectation as his face took on a most evil grin.

'This time, alien, I will have the firepower! Ha ha ha!'

About two hours later Folterknecht set down his flying machine on the roadside just outside Stone. With the flick of a switch, he converted it into an armoured car and drove to the town's big hotel. The road took him past Kunnikunde's castle, which he could see sitting on a distant hilltop. *That's what I need,* Folterknecht told himself, *a castle! When I've taken over this town, that castle will be mine!*

The current owner of the castle was at that moment living in her own dream world. She was waist-deep in thousand-dollar notes and almost delirious with joy. The devil had filled her bedroom with money to keep her busy for a while. She had been frantically collecting it by hand for what seemed like hours and didn't seem to be making any progress. Then she had an idea. A little while later, her servants delivered a powerful leaf vacuum and fifty large empty bags to her room. It worked brilliantly. Within an hour her bedroom was stacked with forty-nine full bags of money and one half full.

Kunnikunde was already well on the way to losing her mind, but this half-empty bag of money seemed to push her over the edge. 'That miser, Lucifer,' she wailed, 'left me with one bag only half full! Is that fair? How could anyone treat an old broke widow like that? It's cruel and brutal! What's the world coming to?'

As quickly as she went into her tantrum she just as quickly came out of it. Kunnikunde, still disguised as the chubby woman with the mean piggy eyes, carefully locked her bedroom door, descended the staircase, strode through the entrance hall and out the front door, headed for the Stone township. In a poor Teutonian accent, she yelled at the top of her voice, '*IIK MUSS ALLES MAKKEN?*' If Werner Little Werner had been there, he would have known exactly what it meant because he'd heard it so many times before: 'MUST I DO EVERYTHING MYSELF?'

Now without his secret police henchman by his side, Dr Folterknecht was doing everything himself too. When he walked into the lobby of the big hotel, the manager, Mr Vogelfutter, greeted him enthusiastically. 'Dr Folterknecht! How nice to see you again!' He was obviously unaware that the secret police boss was now a former secret police boss and a very recent inmate of the Stone Insane Asylum. 'Are you in town for Count Johann Ritter von Krumm's birthday party tomorrow?'

'No time for chit chat, Vogelfutter!' barked the mad doctor. 'I'm here on a secret mission. So secret that even my own colleagues must not know that I'm here. Understood ... yah?'

'Of course. Of course!' an excited Vogelfutter answered and proceeded to tell the doctor that his laboratory in the cellar was still in good order and untouched since his visit last year.

Dr Folterknecht seemed highly pleased with this news. He also suddenly became very interested in the big birthday party that would take place the next evening.

'Will children be attending this von Krumm party?' he asked as casually as he could.

'Yes indeed, doctor!' Vogelfutter happily told him as he moved off to attend to some other guests.

Folterknecht had to contain a squeal of delight. *Perfect timing, yah!* he told himself. And as soon as the manager was out of earshot, he exclaimed aloud, 'And this time there'll be no more Mr Nice Guy, yah!' He rubbed his hands together continuously as he hurried down to his laboratory in the hotel cellar.

19

By this stage, Piggy Kunnikunde had reached Mr Werner Little Werner's house with the intention of destroying him with her iron fist and then stealing all his money and valuables. *Including the money Lucifer gave him!* she reminded herself. *My money!*

Kunnikunde positioned herself on the other side of the street, directly opposite Werner's front door. She lined up her aim at the spot where she estimated the little weasel's head would be when he opened the door and waited for Werner to appear. It wasn't a long wait. Less than ten minutes later he opened the door. Kunnikunde immediately launched her deadly iron fist right on target.

Unfortunately for Kunnikunde, at that very instant a farmer's tractor, towing a huge tank of liquid manure, drove past. Her iron fist smashed a big hole in the tank, almost bursting out the other side. Kunnikunde tried to retract her fist from the tank, but it was stuck fast. In desperation, she tried again but to no avail.

When Werner had turned back towards the street after locking his front door, he was dumbfounded to see the disguised countess being dragged along behind a tractor towing a big tank spewing a horrible dark liquid out of a hole in its side, much of it coating Kunnikunde in the process. It was a sorry and disgusting sight.

As the tank dragging Kunnikunde continued past Werner, now standing on the footpath, he got a whiff of what the horrible dark fluid was, and he also got a close-up view of what was actually going on. Immediately suspicious of the countess, he jumped to the correct conclusion that she had accidentally smashed her iron fist into the tank from directly opposite his house. 'That iron fist was meant for me!' he yelled after Kunnikunde, shaking his own fist. 'You tried to kill me!' He rushed over to his car in a great hurry to get to the church and tell the devil reverend of this murderous attempt on his life.

Werner roared away up the road in the opposite direction to the tractor, which trundled on its way. It took the farmer quite a while before he realised he'd lost nearly half of his smelly liquid, which he planned to spread over his field as fertiliser. When he finally stopped and stepped down from his tractor, he was horrified at the mess he'd left behind. His horror turned to shock when he saw a large clump of the mess at the side of his tank come to life and form into some kind of person, like a *Creature from the Black Lagoon*. When the farmer saw this manure creature pulling something from a hole in the side of his tank, he started yelling. 'What have you done to my tank? You've wasted half my load of manure!'

He started towards the manure creature, but when he saw its eyes so full of hate, he stopped in his tracks, seriously frightened. He jumped back on his tractor and drove off towards his fields in a state of terror. If he'd dared to look back, he would have seen the manure creature walking off in the direction of the town.

Already in town, in the cellar of the big hotel, Dr Folterknecht had just finished inspecting his old laboratory and found everything to his satisfaction. He changed into a spare black suit he had left there a year earlier and left the cellar. His first priority was to find a secure and secluded place to park his strange drone car. He began driving around town checking out potential spots. He eventually found the perfect place to hide the bizarre vehicle. Behind the church was a single parking bay that couldn't be seen from any street. After parking the drone car and locking it, the doctor decided to inspect the church.

He entered through the rear door and snuck up the stairs to the mezzanine level where the organ was located. From this vantage point, he had a clear view of the whole church. He very quietly moved the organ stool close to the balustrade and sat down to watch and listen. He'd only been settled a couple of minutes when he heard something worth listening to. Right below him, a highly agitated Mr Werner Little Werner was bleating loudly to the Reverend Semmelmeier.

'Master ... I think she really did try to kill me,' Werner cried. 'If it wasn't for that farmer driving his—'

Werner didn't finish his sentence. It was cut off by the front door bursting open and a woman's voice screaming out, 'Die, Werner, die!'

Werner, the devil reverend, and Dr Folterknecht right above them, looked around to see a bizarre figure who appeared to be covered with some sort of mud. The instant the breeze from the open door behind the figure reached their nostrils, they realised it wasn't mud.

The manure-coated Kunnikunde immediately launched her iron fist at Little Werner's head with full-blooded vengeance and precision accuracy. It would almost certainly have killed him if the devil reverend hadn't once again caught her fist inches in front of Werner's face. The devil's fury at Kunnikunde transformed him into his hideous werewolf-like self, right in full view of Dr Folterknecht. The mad doctor almost fell backwards off the organ stool with shock. He was then astounded to see the now hideous-looking Reverend Semmelmeier move from his position below him to where the manure-covered woman was standing, about thirty feet away, in just the blink of an eye!

Yet again, the devil reverend went ballistic at the psychotic Kunnikunde. 'Can I ever trust you, you ridiculous, stupid woman?' Folterknecht heard him shouting. 'Can you not stick to a simple plan? Can you not wait until tomorrow evening when your goal will be achieved? Can you not trust me to make it happen? Obviously, you can't, so I have no choice but to act!'

The devil reverend began waving his hands in front of Kunnikunde's face and staring into her eyes said, 'You are a little girl now! A lovely little girl! Nice Uncle Werner will take you home, give you a shower and put you into bed, where you will sleep soundly until Uncle Werner wakes you up.'

The hypnotised Kunnikunde immediately tried to hug nice Uncle Werner. All the way to the castle he desperately attempted to avoid the foul-smelling countess's advances by staying as far ahead of her as possible. On arrival at the castle gates, they saw Mr Broombridge on crutches about to struggle into a waiting taxi.

'Mr Broombridge, I love you!' Kunnikunde cried out in delight, rushing up and giving him a big hug.

It all happened very quickly. Kunnikunde was vigorously embracing Broombridge before he could move, which he couldn't have done very quickly on crutches anyway. He just stood there in utter astonishment. Then he got a whiff of the ugly, foul-smelling liquid now smeared all over the front of his previously immaculate suit. 'Why me?' he wailed. 'Why always me?'

The taxi driver also got a strong whiff through his open window. As Mr Broombridge attempted to climb into the taxi, the driver yelled, 'Stop! You're not getting into my taxi covered in all that poo.' With that he drove off, leaving a dumbfounded Broombridge wobbling precariously on his crutches, somehow just managing to keep his balance and, for once, avoiding further injury. He was forced to go back into the castle to shower and change before getting another taxi to take him to the big hotel.

Little Werner and the hypnotised Kunnikunde were already inside. Werner had to get Kunnikunde to take three showers before she was properly cleaned up. The devil's hypnosis was working well because once the countess was finally in bed, she fell asleep immediately.

Werner took the chance to extract enough from Kunnikunde's massive bags of money to pay the castle staff, something she would never have done. Her usual tactic was to fire people a day or so before their pay was due. Werner also filled his pockets and a pillowcase with thousand-dollar notes just for himself and then he left.

20

The deranged Dr Folterknecht snuck back out of the church shaking with excitement. Hearing Werner call Semmelmeier "master" and witnessing the reverend's extraordinary behaviour, convinced him that Reverend Semmelmeier was the head alien responsible for infesting children and adults alike to use them in conquering the world.

The doctor rushed back to his laboratory at the big hotel to prepare for his next move. It was unfortunate timing; he narrowly avoided running into five Teutonian Secret Police officers at the front entrance. He ducked behind a pillar until they'd disappeared inside, and then found a side door into the hotel. Once in his laboratory in the cellar, he quickly made a sign saying, WARNING! POISONOUS GASES INSIDE. TO ENTER SAFELY, DO IT CAUTIOUSLY, ONE AT A TIME! He affixed it to the door and waited. Just minutes later he heard the synchronised footsteps of the five secret policemen approaching his laboratory. They stopped and read the sign. As disciplined officers, they followed the sign's instructions and entered in single file, making it easy for Dr Folterknecht, hiding behind the door, to fire tranquilliser darts into each of their backsides. Seconds later they were all unconscious on the floor, and he tied them up.

The mad doctor's hypnosis technique was completely different from that of the devil's. Folterknecht used an electronic method. He systematically wired the five police officers to his mind-altering machine with the intention of making them loyal to him again.

At the church, Werner was also involved in some mind-altering shenanigans as he helped the devil reverend prepare a big batch of special cookies for the holy meal he was going to bless at the party the next day.

The devil explained that anyone who ate one of the cookies would be under his spell. Then, on his signal, they would all try to kill Johann Ritter von Krumm and his wife and son.

'Killing is an art,' the devil said, repeating his favourite mantra. 'Tomorrow there will be deaths of innocent people and other innocent people will rot in jail for crimes they did not commit! This, for me, is the ultimate entertainment. Ha ha ha!'

All the devil's talk of killing reminded Werner that he was still in shock about Kunnikunde trying to kill him. He pleaded with his new master to take her killing power away.

'Yes, Werner ... can do and will do. I can't work with her anymore. Although I have to say, I quite like her untrustworthiness and that her heart is so full of evil and hate, but she is impossible to control. So, after the big party tomorrow, and the killing is done, I will turn Countess Kunnikunde von Krumm back into the common thief she was born as. No more lethal iron fist, just a basic pilfering arm extending to no more than five metres with which she can continue her petty, thieving ways.'

'Thank you, master! Thank you, master!' Werner cried, grovelling before the devil reverend and kissing his hand profusely.

'Enough, Werner!' the devil reverend growled. 'Get some sleep tonight; you have a very busy day tomorrow.'

21

Andy was already asleep, fully clothed, on Michaela's orders. Michaela had turned back into the magic pencil to rest before the next day's action. Even the devil was resting. Rather than sleeping, though, he was floating above the altar communicating with his network of assistant devils and spirit demons throughout his universe of evil. Kunnikunde was still in a deep hypnotic sleep. It was a quiet night in Stone.

As usual, Commander Wurstling was enjoying a sound, restful night's sleep, which was lucky because what greeted him at his office first thing next morning was anything but restful. He was confronted by a long queue of angry citizens complaining about a line of poo on their street. The stench, they said, was unbearable, and they demanded an immediate clean-up. Wurstling relished this situation because crime was virtually non-existent in Stone. This wasn't just a clean-up, he told himself; he could smell a criminal investigation.

'I will investigate!' he proudly announced. 'I will find the guilty party!'

The people weren't particularly interested in that; they just wanted the poo cleaned up.

'In the meantime,' he yelled, so they could all hear him, 'no removal of the evidence is allowed!'

This was precisely what the citizens did not want to hear, but Wurstling was already marching off to solve the poo crime. Sergeant Fritzel hurried after him and the crowd decided to tag along as well, sensing the prospect of some free entertainment.

When they reached the seemingly endless trail of poo, Sergeant Fritzel sensibly suggested that it looked like a tank of manure had sprung a leak as it was being towed along the street, probably by a tractor being driven by a farmer.

Wurstling reacted angrily to his sergeant's theory and told him off.

'A real detective like me,' he proclaimed loudly, 'has to investigate every aspect of the case step by step and must avoid jumping to easy conclusions. The poo line starts right here,' he barked, pointing at the ground and then at a house. 'See that, Sergeant? The line starts right here in front of Little Werner's house, you fool, Fritzel! Is Werner a farmer? Does he own a tank and a tractor? I don't think so! Forget your farmer culprit, Sergeant!' He pointed again at Werner's house. 'In there we'll find our likely suspect!'

Wurstling stormed across to Werner's front door and banged on it heavily, several times. 'Open up! This is the Teutonian Police!' he yelled.

When Werner opened the door and saw Commander Wurstling and about twenty other people scowling at him, he looked very confused.

'What kind of laxatives are you taking, Mr Little Werner, to make such a mess pooing on a public road?' Wurstling thundered. 'Don't you know that pooing in public is forbidden in Teutonia?'

Werner, so deeply outraged and insulted in front of all these people by such a revolting and ridiculous suggestion, he was gasping for air trying to get his words out. 'Wurstling! Wurstling you buffoon!' he finally managed to shriek. 'How dare you accuse me of something I had nothing to do with! I certainly did not punch a hole with an iron fist into the side of the farmer's manure tank!' The last sentence just slipped out; the look on Werner's face suggested he was already regretting saying it.

Sergeant Fritzel dared not looked pleased with himself for his earlier, accurate assessment of the crime because his boss was looking ready to explode with confusion and frustration after what he'd heard.

'Mr Little Werner is right,' one older lady among the onlookers piped up. She then proceeded to give a very detailed account of what she observed. 'I saw a chubby woman being dragged along the road by the tank that farmer Dungenfeld was towing behind his tractor. She was attached by a funny-looking cord and was gradually pulling herself by the cord towards the tank. The cord was coming out of a hole in the tank. Liquid manure was leaking out of that hole and splashing all over the woman being dragged along behind. At the very moment she pulled herself right up to the side of the tank, below the hole in the side, the farmer jumped on the brakes and brought his tractor to a halt. The sudden stop caused a huge amount of liquid manure to gush from the hole in the tank, completely swamping the poor woman hanging onto the cord. She then raised herself out of that evil, foul-smelling mess, pulled something out of the hole in the tank and headed off on foot towards town.'

Commander Wurstling almost burst a boiler. 'You were an eyewitness?' he shouted. 'Why didn't you tell me this before?'

Before the lady could answer, they were all distracted by a loud whirring noise slowly increasing in volume. It seemed to be coming from an approaching tractor, which stopped right in front of Werner's house. It was farmer Dungenfeld, who had built himself a kind of vacuum machine attached to his tractor. The machine had sucked up all the evil liquid from the road.

When the farmer jumped off his tractor, he stormed straight over to the commander, who was speechless with anger that all the smelly evidence had disappeared.

Wurstling didn't get a chance to berate Dungenfeld because the farmer was already shouting at the top of his voice, 'I've been attacked by farmers in the next town! They tried to sabotage my superior crop by destroying my tank of special liquid fertiliser! They are jealous! They are the culprits! This time they didn't just send drones to spy on my crops but some strange demon that launched some sort of missile into my manure tank, creating a gaping hole. This manure is liquid gold for my crops, and they tried to steal it! Commander Wurstling, you must go at once to the next town and arrest every farmer there!'

Once again, the baffled commander didn't get a chance to respond because the crowd of people began clapping and cheering farmer Dungenfeld for removing the stinking mess from their street.

'Noodlehead!' Wurstling yelled at the farmer when the wild applause finally stopped. 'Is your brain the size of a peanut? You have removed important state evidence, you fool!'

'He put it there, so he should be allowed to remove it!' a voice in the crowd called out.

'Cleaning up your own mess is not a crime!' another voice declared.

The crowd cheered its agreement and began to disperse, happy with the outcome.

For the commander, the case was becoming more and more complicated and being forced to think agitated him. 'Sergeant Fritzel,' he commanded, 'please get a written statement from that eyewitness and find out why there's a fist-shaped hole in farmer Dungenfeld's manure tank. Looks like a smuggling operation to me.' With that he turned on his heel and stalked back to his office, looking forward to enjoying the big fat sausage roll awaiting him there. Also awaiting him were six men, all dressed in black with red ties.

Dr Folterknecht stepped forward. 'Commander, we need to see you!' he demanded. 'We will need your assistance in arresting an imposter!'

'Give me two minutes,' Wurstling said, 'then come to my office.' So saying, he walked straight past them, went into his office and closed the door behind him. When he sat down at his desk, he noticed that the light on his GPS-controlled secret alarm was shining red. Now, this was an alarm only required in the most dangerous situations and must have been triggered by Helga, his trusted secretary, with good reason.

22

Trying to keep his calm, Commander Wurstling opened his office door and leaned out. 'Folterknecht!' he barked. 'Come in ... and please ask my secretary to come in too.' He put the alarm control in his pocket, then took his big police revolver out of a draw, placed it conspicuously on his desk, and sat down. As it happened, the commander was actually anti-guns and nearly everyone in Stone knew that his revolver was either empty or filled with blanks. To anyone unfamiliar with the police chief, however, the big revolver would have looked threatening indeed.

As Folterknecht entered Wurstling's office, he hesitated at the sight of the stern-looking commander and the big revolver.

When Wurstling asked why his secretary Helga hadn't come in, Folterknecht explained that seeing as the commander was busy with visitors, she had taken the opportunity to go shopping for half an hour.

'Folterknecht!' Wurstling growled. 'Should I find any irregular behaviour from you and your people, I will be forced to use my gun! I will first shoot you in the foot! Then in the knee! Then I will turn nasty!'

'There is nothing to worry about, Commander!' Folterknecht hastily assured him. 'All I want you to do is arrest the imposter,

Reverend Semmelmeier. We will do the rest by sedating him.' The doctor slowly rubbed his hands together, trying to ensure the excitement making him tremble inside didn't show on the outside. His hand rubbing rapidly got faster and faster and his eyes started to pop as he was becoming increasingly impatient with the police chief. It also gave the impression he was rapidly becoming unhinged.

Wurstling jumped up from his seat. *This Folterknecht is a basket-case!* he thought. 'You must be out of your mind, Folterknecht,' he shouted. 'Reverend Semmelmeier has been the pastor of the church here for over forty years! He is definitely not an imposter of any kind! What a ridiculous idea!'

'He is an alien!' screamed the crazy doctor. 'I saw it myself!' With that, he gave a slight hand gesture and suddenly the police chief had five guns aimed at his head. 'No more Mr Nice Guy, Wurstling!' Folterknecht shouted. 'You will follow my orders and do what I tell you, you ignorant fool!'

Minutes later, they marched Wurstling out of the police station and headed for the church. As all this was going on, Sergeant Fritzel had been following the muddy footprints of what he believed was the demon that had damaged farmer Dungenfeld's manure tank. The prints were very confusing for him because one foot seemed to be that of a man's boot and the other a woman's shoe.

When he got close to the church entrance, he saw Mr Little Werner with a big hose washing away manure footprints Kunnikunde had left on the footpath leading up to the church door.

'Stop! Police! Halt!' the sergeant shouted, not yet aware of his commander marching towards the church with the evil crew of the Teutonian Secret Police. He was totally focused on stopping Werner from messing with the trail of manure footprints. He certainly wasn't expecting to hear his boss's voice at that moment.

'Sergeant Fritzel!' Wurstling shouted. 'Everything is OK, OK, OK!'

The surprised Fritzel started walking towards his commander and the six men in black suits and red ties.

'Sergeant ... you fool!' Wurstling shouted again. 'I said OK three times!'

The sergeant froze. He suddenly remembered that 'OK' three times was the code for 'highest danger,' and he was meant to take cover immediately. He desperately launched himself towards a large metal bin nearby, half a second too late.

'Karl-Otto, shoot him!' Dr Folterknecht ordered, and a poisonous dart hit Sergeant Fritzel in the backside as he jumped over the bin and disappeared behind it.

'Onwards!' commanded Folterknecht, and the group continued marching towards the church.

Observing this incident, Little Werner stopped hosing down the manure footprints and ran into the church to warn his master, locking the front door behind him.

Half a minute later Folterknecht was banging on the door. 'Open up, please, Semmelmeier!' he demanded. 'I have the Teutonian Secret Police with me ... we need to talk to you!'

He barely finished his sentence when the front door opened to reveal a smiling Devil Reverend Semmelmeier holding a silver tray of black cookies.

Commander Wurstling pushed his way past the reverend with Folterknecht close behind him, followed by the five secret police officers. The devil reverend stepped in front of the officers and offered them black cookies. 'These holy cookies will cleanse your souls and bring you closer to your God,' he said.

Each officer instinctively took one and ate it as they continued after Folterknecht into the church. The reverend then offered Wurstling and Folterknecht a cookie each, but both declined.

'Semmelmeier!' barked Commander Wurstling, gesturing towards Folterknecht. 'This lunatic here believes that you are some kind of alien, which I find ridiculous. Please assure him that you are no such thing!'

'Of course,' responded the reverend, his face suddenly wobbling like a bowl of jelly. 'Get out of here, Wurstling!' he cried. 'And close the church. I'm possessed by the—'

He didn't finish the sentence. His body raised itself about a foot above the floor as he spread his arms wide and turned around. 'Sleep ... sleep ... sleeeeeep,' he murmured, as if in a trance. He quickly recovered, but he was still floating just above the floor.

'Do you see that, you incompetent buffoon?' Dr Folterknecht yelled at Commander Wurstling, pointing frantically at the floating reverend. 'Do you see that, you poor excuse for a policeman ... walking around with an unloaded gun? Do you see that?'

Wurstling's response was to take ten steps back and position himself closer to a side door. That triggered Folterknecht to make his move.

'Karl-Otto, open fire!' he yelled. At the same time, with an evil smile, he aimed his own gun at Reverend Semmelmeier, thinking he was an alien, having no idea it was actually Lucifer. At exactly this moment, the devil showed his true being and with a flick of his hand sent Folterknecht's gun flying out of his hand at high speed. It hit the floor and slid down the aisle towards the back of the church with the doctor in hot pursuit, the devil's hand slapping him hard as he went. The five secret policemen were on their knees calling out, 'Master! Master!' all having succumbed to the hallucinatory effects of the black cookies they'd eaten.

23

The sound of sirens could be heard in the distance, rapidly getting louder and louder as police reinforcements raced to the scene, locked onto the secret GPS-alarm-system locator Wurstling had in his pocket.

Something in another pocket had also proved very useful. The poisonous dart fired into Sergeant Fritzel's backside had actually hit the secret hipflask of schnapps he always carried in his back pocket. Originally panicked when the dart hit him, the sergeant was now surprised to find he was still conscious and uninjured. The approaching sirens snapped him into action, and he crept unseen up to the church's side entrance. While not a naturally brave man, the thought that his commander might be in danger crowded out any fears he had. As he was about to open the side door, it burst open, crashing into Sergeant Fritzel and sending him backwards onto the ground. Commander Wurstling rushed out, almost stumbling over the dazed sergeant.

'Not time to sleep, Sergeant!' he shouted. 'This is an emergency!'

Fritzel managed to drag himself to his feet, the bruising on his face already showing black and blue.

'Around to the front door, now!' Wurstling yelled as he ran full tilt along the side of the church. 'We have to warn our colleagues; they're arriving now!'

His words were all but drowned out by the blaring sirens of the numerous police vehicles screeching to a halt outside the church.

Inside, Dr Folterknecht retrieved his gun and rushed out the back door, racing as fast as he could to his car. He quickly reversed out of his secluded parking space and set his armoured car in flight mode, transforming it back into a drone. He hovered just above ground level waiting for the five secret police officers to arrive—but not to give them a lift. He didn't have to wait long. Three of them burst out the back door but instantly fell to the ground in a hail of darts fired by Folterknecht. The other two stayed under cover behind the door, trying to shoot his drone down. Their revolver bullets had no effect on the armoured drone. Folterknecht took off, shooting at anything that moved. He zoomed around to the front of the church and opened fire on the newly arrived policemen as they clambered out of their vehicles, taking out seven of them.

Cries of 'officer down!' rang out as the police returned fire at Folterknecht's drone and tried to help their fallen colleagues.

Inside the church, the devil went into action. With a wave of his hand, he woke the three secret police officers downed by Folterknecht and telehopped them into the church. Together with Werner, he formed a circle of four holding hands and teleported them to Kunnikunde's castle. He told them to stay there until five o'clock then to wake Kunnikunde and return to the church, bringing Kunnikunde with them. A split second later, the devil, in his Reverend Semmelmeier guise, was back in the church kneeling in front of the altar.

Commander Wurstling's secretary, Helga, having recovered from being hit by a tranquilliser dart, rushed to the church. She found Wurstling taking cover behind a large pillar with his eyes closed. Helga showed him a wanted poster for Dr Folterknecht which read, DANGER! INSANE! APPROACH WITH UTMOST CAUTION!

'I knew it!' shouted the commander. 'I knew it!'

He waved the poster at Sergeant Fritzel. 'Go into the church and arrest this man immediately, Sergeant!'

'But, Commander,' Fritzel cried, 'the doctor flew away in his drone!'

'What?' barked Wurstling. 'You let him escape? Inexcusable, Fritzel! And why are all these police officers sleeping on the ground? This is totally unacceptable behaviour! Do I have to do everything myself?' With that he stormed up to the open front door of the church, closely followed by Sergeant Fritzel and four policemen. Wurstling stepped inside and yelled, 'Semmelmeier! We need to talk!'

The policemen found the church empty except for the reverend, who was kneeling at the altar, seemingly praying.

The commander strode right up behind him, while his colleagues scoured the church. 'Semmelmeier!' Wurstling roared in the reverend's ear. 'What is going on here? Where have all the people gone?'

'A demon! A demon!' wailed the reverend. 'A demon tried to take over my mind! Terrible! You saw him! You must find him and lock him up!'

'But, Semmelmeier,' Wurstling barked, 'I saw you disarm him from a great distance and—with all respect—you were floating in the air!'

'Illusions! Illusions!' the reverend cried. 'He was using toxic gases which make you see things that aren't real! The manipulative capacity of a demon is great! This is a police matter and has nothing to do with the church!'

'Hmmm,' the commander replied, trying to think, which made him agitated. 'OK, everyone out! The fugitive has escaped. But I will still keep an eye on you, Semmelmeier,' he threatened as he started to leave. 'Consider yourself on my watch list.'

One the way back to the police station, Commander Wurstling came up with an idea that would eventually help to mess up the devil's plan, although that wasn't the police chief's intention. He remembered the words of the reverend at the beginning of their encounter. "Close the church," he had said. However, even though he was head of the local police, the commander had no authority to close the church without a very good reason. The suspicion of black magic and demons was not enough. Then something else the reverend had said sparked an idea. There could be safety implications for parishioners. The protection of his fellow citizens was certainly a very good reason to close the church.

Back at the police station, the commander and his men prepared and printed two different kinds of posters. One was a wanted poster with Dr Folterknecht's picture on it; the other was a danger alert with the words, WARNING! WARNING! HIGHLY DANGEROUS TOXIC GASES HAVE BEEN DETECTED IN OUR CHURCH! STAY AWAY! Both clearly displayed the commander's signature of authority.

Police officers then strategically placed the posters all over town, and especially around the perimeter of the church.

Now at last, with the opportunity to eat his sausage roll in peace, Commander Wurstling found it even more enjoyable because he could admire his signature on the posters as he happily munched away. *The first posters with my signature on them!* he told himself proudly.

24

At that same moment, Dr Folterknecht was also talking to himself. '*Schweine hund!*' he shouted with rage.

After escaping in his flying machine, the mad doctor made one pretty bad mistake. On his way to the big barn where Johann's birthday party would be held, he flew over farmer Dungenfeld's field. This was a farmer constantly on the alert for spying drones, so Dungenfeld didn't hesitate to fire his shotgun at Folterknecht's flying machine as it passed overhead. A full load of pellets penetrated the drone's seat and into the doctor's backside. It was at this precise moment that he shouted the words, '*Schweine hund!*'

Those were the last words farmer Dungenfeld heard before he was hit in his own backside by one of Folterknecht's darts and collapsed to the ground unconscious.

Still cursing under his breath and squirming in his seat, the doctor could see the big barn just ahead of him. He circled it several times to get the lay of the land and then landed at the side of a nearby road. He immediately turned his flying machine into an armoured car again and drove it to the barn, where he had picked out the perfect parking spot from the air. He stopped the car between two big catering trucks, where his car would be hidden, but he would still have a good view of the barn and its surrounding area. 'Ha ha ha!' he gloated. 'All I have to do is wait!'

With numerous shotgun pellets embedded in his backside, it wasn't a comfortable wait, so he took the first aid kit from the glove box and attempted to remove the pellets and treat the wounds. He wasn't entirely successful, but he'd put up with worse in the past ... especially the large syringe of truth serum antidote injected deep into his nose a year earlier.

Andy and the magic pencil were deep in conversation, although no one could hear them because, as they often did, they were communicating telepathically. The only time they spoke to one another out loud was when the pencil assumed the human form of Michaela.

Johann had returned from his business trip earlier that morning. He was greeted enthusiastically by all, especially Sassy who almost bowled him over twice in her excitement at seeing him again.

'What are you feeding this dog? She's getting heavier by the day,' Johann called out before embracing Anna, who wished him a happy birthday.

Andy rushed downstairs and gave his dad a big hug. 'Happy birthday, Dad!'

'Thanks, son,' Johann said, hugging Andy hard in return. He looked around. 'Where is that girl? I'm starting to get used to having her around.'

'I'm here, sir. Happy birthday,' Johann heard in his thoughts.

'Ah, just a voice in my head,' he said. 'That's good! In that case, we should have a quiet and peaceful celebration tonight.'

The magic pencil made no comment, which pleased Johann and he started to relax.

On a street in a less affluent part of town, the village drunk had been found totally comatose and was being carried directly to the hospital. He had found the hip flask Sergeant Fritzel had dropped after it was struck by a poisonous dart. The drunk had taken one sip from it and collapsed to the ground, instantly unconscious, still clutching the flask tightly in one hand. The head nurse attending him finally wrested it from his grip and sniffed it briefly to determine what kind of liquid it contained. A split second later, she fainted. A second nurse who also sniffed the flask met the same fate. When the doctor came in and saw the two nurses down, he called the toxicology department to come and remove the flask. Within minutes the two nurses recovered, complaining of slight headaches. When the drunkard finally awoke, he was ready to swear off alcohol for the rest of his life.

25

As he sat watching from his armoured car parked between the catering trucks, Folterknecht saw Andy slowly walking towards the big barn. What he couldn't see, of course, was the pencil in Andy's front pocket, from which Andy had just removed the top cap.

But the doctor did have a clear view of the caterers busily preparing the buffet dinner. There were huge bowls filled with salad, vast amounts of sausages and pork chops being carried to the barbecues, and many crates of beer and wine going to the huge bar.

Out of Folterknecht's view, inside the barn, the florist was arranging beautiful bouquets of flowers on each table, while suspended above her, covering the entire ceiling, was a giant net of balloons all set to be released at precisely the right moment. Up on the stage the oompah band members were setting up, ready for their big performance.

Meanwhile, the magic pencil had positioned Andy and his friends, Hartmuth, Jurgen and Hansi, in the forest opposite the big barn. It gave them a good view of what was going on without anyone seeing them while the pencil issued instructions.

'Pssst!' the pencil said, speaking to all of them in their thoughts only. 'Hartmuth, I want you at all times to stick like glue to Reverend Semmelmeier. Should he have a tray or plate of cookies with him, play clumsy and bump it so hard that all his cookies fall on the floor. Then, Jurgen and Hansi, you step on them and crush as many as you can. And should he have a bag, snatch it from his hands and run out the back entrance and hide. Understood?'

The three boys nodded excitedly.

'Andy, the first guests arrive at six o'clock, which is only about an hour away. We have lots of work to do before then.'

At exactly five o'clock, the devil reverend opened the church for his holy meal celebration prior to Johann's big party. He planned to hand out as many of his devilish cookies as he could. He was surprised to find no one waiting outside to come in but remained optimistic they would soon start arriving for the free food. To occupy himself until then, he went back inside and began playing Chopin's 'Funeral March' on the pipe organ—it was his favourite song. He enjoyed his own playing so much that he lost track of the time. When he finally stopped, he quickly grabbed a large silver tray of cookies to hand out to his flock. To his consternation, there was no flock, only old Mrs Rottweiler who had left her glasses at home and hadn't read the warning posters about the toxic gases in the church.

'AAAARRRRGGGGH!' screamed the devil reverend, glaring furiously at Mrs Rottweiler. 'Only one silly, decrepit old woman is here to take holy meal! What is happening in this unholy, godforsaken town! Get out, old woman, before I throw you out!'

The devil reverend's outburst proved to be particularly bad timing. Right at that moment, Lady Heger-Steel was entering the open church door, holding a handkerchief over her mouth and nose. Walking past the church on her way to the party, she had seen Mrs Rottweiler go inside. Realising that the old lady probably hadn't read the toxic gas warning signs, she decided to go into the church and warn her.

As Lady Heger-Steel stepped inside the front door, she heard everything Reverend Semmelmeier screamed at dear old Mrs Rottweiler. Her outrage was terrifying to witness! Before the devil reverend knew what had happened, he was airborne with the silver tray of cookies catapulting out of his hands towards the ceiling. As he landed flat on his back on the floor, the tray came plummeting down and bounced off his head. A second later, the cookies hit the floor and broke into small pieces all around him. His head hurt and a great big red Heger-Steel palm print on the side of his face was throbbing painfully.

Once Lady Heger-Steel had escorted the distressed Mrs Rottweiler from the church, she turned around and yelled at the stunned reverend who was picking himself up off the floor and holding his head with both hands. 'Semmelmeier! Are you possessed by the devil himself? How dare you treat an old lady like that? Outrageous! Unforgivable!'

With that, not realising just how correct she was, Lady Heger-Steel stormed off, almost crashing into a group of seven people heading toward her. They somehow managed to avoid her considerable bulk and went inside the church.

Werner, the five secret policemen and Kunnikunde, still under hypnosis and thinking she was a little girl, saw the devil reverend looking a little dazed and rubbing his head.

'Master!' Werner cried. 'What happened?'

'Never mind,' the devil reverend replied curtly.

'Master, you have been sabotaged!' Werner cried, holding up a poster he had torn down from outside the church.

The devil read the poster warning of toxic gases in the church and rolled his eyes. 'Beaten by a bumbling oaf of a police chief!' he muttered. 'But at least my disguise is still rock solid. Werner, get me some more cookies. We will distribute them in the party tent.'

'Barn, master. Big barn,' Werner said. 'I used to play there when I was a child before it was renovated,' he called back, as he rushed off to get more of the devil's cookies.

When Werner returned a short time later, he proudly announced that he had organised a company bus to take them all to the big barn. 'The board members of the old Ritter von Krumm factory will have to find their own transport!' he laughed.

They all left the church and clambered onto the bus. The devil reverend took the front seat beside Werner, who was driving. The rest sat in the back of the bus. 'I will have to wake Kunnikunde from her hypnotic trance,' the devil said.

'No! Not yet please!' Werner begged, on the verge of panic. 'Not until we get there; otherwise she'll try to kill me right here on the bus!'

The devil reverend just nodded in agreement and Werner leant back in his seat mightily relieved.

'Drive very slowly, Werner,' the devil reverend told him, 'and stop frequently when there are people on the side of the street or at bus stops. I want to pretend to need directions and then hand out my devilish cookies.'

At about the third stop one old lady asked the reverend if he was unwell. Of all the people, she said, he should know the way to the barn because he had performed countless weddings there. The devil was pleased to hear this and started to relax.

'How many cookies have we given out, Werner?' he asked.

'About thirty-two, master.'

'Ha ha ha!' the devil roared. 'That was always the plan. It will be a massacre!' He howled with excitement.

BANG! The bus lurched forward. 'Someone's crashed into the back of us!' Werner exclaimed. Before he could get out of the driver's seat to investigate, Commander Wurstling's angry face appeared at Werner's side window.

'How dare you reverse into a police car?' Wurstling thundered.

'I just stopped!' Werner yelled back. 'I didn't reverse!'

The commander inspected the police vehicle and couldn't find any noticeable damage and calmed down, slightly. 'Drive on ... but don't reverse again!' he shouted.

He got back into the police van and followed the bus down the road at a safe distance.

26

Thirty minutes prior to this incident, the magic pencil turned into Michaela again. Leaving Hartmuth, Jurgen and Hansi hidden out of sight, she and Andy walked slowly from the cover of the forest, moving closer to the entrance of the big barn.

Michaela suddenly stopped dead in her tracks. 'Folterknecht is here somewhere!' she announced. 'I can sense it.' She stood motionless for several seconds before quickly identifying the mad doctor's armoured vehicle between the two catering trucks. 'We really don't need any interference from him,' she said, carefully approaching the vehicle from the back. Then, with just one wave of her hand, Folterknecht and his vehicle disappeared.

'What happened?' Andy gasped.

'I shrank it to the size of a small stone. But it will only last for an hour and a bit.'

'Look! Look!' Andy whispered. 'Mr Broombridge just parked his car in the same spot!'

Andy and Michaela watched as Broombridge and his family exited his very expensive and ostentatious limousine. The meticulous Broombridge was extremely particular about where he parked, always concerned that his precious car might be scratched. To him, the space between the two catering trucks looked completely safe.

As usual, he was perfectly dressed, in a hunting outfit with a beautiful suede jacket. Slowly but surely recovering from his injuries, Broombridge now required only one crutch to get around. Keen to get the best seat in the barn, he hobbled as quickly as he could manage towards the entrance.

'Uh oh!' Andy chuckled, watching Broombridge's clumsy progress with great amusement. 'This won't end well!'

'Vain, fussy, arrogant people are always more accident-prone,' Michaela said. But then she was suddenly all business again. 'Focus, Andy! Ignore all distractions! Focus! And focus again!' She pointed at a large flowerpot near the entrance. 'Have Sassy sit over there and then follow me.'

'Stay right there, Sassy, and don't move until I come back for you,' Andy ordered, then hurried after Michaela.

'My spirits in the devil's mirror,' she explained, 'will now be trying to wake up the real Reverend Semmelmeier more often in order to distract the devil. It will make it more difficult for the Evil One to maintain his disguise.'

As Andy and Michaela entered the barn, a festive atmosphere was building. The oompah band was getting into the swing of things and more and more guests were arriving.

Soon after, the devil and his entourage arrived in their bus with Werner driving ever so slowly. As Michaela had hoped, he pulled up at the furthest end of the car park behind the big barn.

Once everyone had disembarked, they huddled around the devil reverend as he gave them their instructions, speaking very intensely and forcefully. 'In exactly one hour, we will strike! Everyone is to take their positions exactly as discussed! I'll run through it one last time! Werner, you and three secret policemen will cover the front entrance. You other two will stay with me at the back entrance. As a group, you are my prime killing machines! The thirty-two guests who ate my cookies will enhance the massacre, even though they don't carry any weapons.'

He looked at Kunnikunde who was standing gawping around and grinning like an idiot, still under the impression she was a little girl.

'I will now wake Kunnikunde from her hypnotic trance and place her in the right position.'

'Please wait until I'm at the front entrance!' Werner squealed. 'I don't trust her! She is insane and will try to kill me!' With that, he rushed off towards the front of the barn as quickly as his short legs would take him.

The devil reverend led Kunnikunde to a position in the car park he had chosen that would make an ideal vantage point for her to observe the goings-on in the barn.

He was about to wake Kunnikunde from her trance when he was interrupted by a loud cheer from the people inside. Johann and Anna had entered the front door to the accompaniment of the band playing 'Happy Birthday.' Everybody stood up and clapped and cheered until the couple had taken their seats.

When the wild applause finally abated, the devil brought Kunnikunde out of her hypnotic trance. She was instantly back to her usual obnoxious self. He immediately started to read her the riot act.

'Kunnikunde!' he hissed. 'Can you for once in your life be a team player and not jeopardise our carefully thought-out plan? Can you restrain yourself for once and not use your iron fist until I explicitly order you to do so?'

'Of course,' answered Kunnikunde, looking a little confused. 'Where are we? I don't know this place.'

'At your brother-in-law's big barn building,' the devil reverend replied impatiently. 'Just remember what I said ... follow my orders and nothing else!' He started growling. 'Any mistake—even the smallest one—and I will take away your powers! And not only that ... I will take away all your money as well. You will really be the poor broke widow you claim to be! Understood?'

'Not my money!' whimpered Kunnikunde. 'I want more money, not less! Money! Money!'

'I don't care what you want!' the devil snarled.

'But—'

'No buts!' the devil shrieked. 'Just do as you're told! This is your position. You're to stay put until I tell you otherwise!' He abruptly turned on his heels and walked towards the back of the barn, leaving Kunnikunde shaking her head as she watched him go.

'Idiot!' she muttered under her breath. 'What an idiot!'

Kunnikunde turned her attention to the new barn, and through the big windows, she could clearly see the fun and festivities going on inside. At the thought of Johann having the time of his life, her insane jealousy took over. She became totally focused on eliminating her brother-in-law and his family. 'Destroying your business and shunning you from the family is not good enough!' she hissed to herself. 'Death is the only satisfactory solution!' She readied herself to employ her deadly fist. 'The devil can go to hell!' she cried, then chuckled at her own unintentional joke. 'His complex, carefully thought-out plan is ridiculous, unnecessary ... and just plain stupid! Not to mention laughably over-complicated. Keep it simple, stupid! Three quick strikes with my fist and that lousy family is dead! A simple, foolproof and effective plan!'

27

As Kunnikunde marched off to enact her plan, the devil reverend was nearing the rear entrance of the barn. He paused to scan his surroundings.

Observing him from the cover of some bushes, Andy and Michaela were willing him to continue. 'He's only half a metre from the invisible trap you've set for him!' Andy murmured in frustration.

'Just a couple of steps forward, Evil One,' Michaela whispered. When the devil still hadn't moved after a long, tense minute, Michaela nudged Andy. 'Walk past him into the barn and take your position. Then in exactly three minutes, take off your jacket.'

As Andy walked past the devil reverend, he slightly, and unintentionally, bumped him as he went by.

'Oh, sorry, Reverend Semmelmeier!' Andy exclaimed.

'Not at all,' the devil reverend replied with a pleasant smile. 'Go to your parents, my son. The show is just about to begin.'

The moment Andy took his position inside the barn, he was greeted by his three friends.

'Andy,' Jurgen said anxiously, 'the devil must have somehow given his cookies to people before they got here!'

'How do you know?'

'Because a lot of them have been complaining of getting a very bitter taste in their mouths soon after they arrived,' Hartmuth added.

'It made them feel sick,' Hansi said. 'Most had to run to the toilet to throw up!'

Andy smiled. He realised that it must have been a trick by Michaela to defuse the drugs in the devil's cookies. 'Just relax for now but stay focused and be ready to follow any of Michaela's instructions.'

Just outside, the devil reverend was still standing motionless, now scanning the barn building itself, his eyes glowing red. He was looking for any flaws in the construction, which would tell him that it had been built by humans and not by spiritual forces. He quickly detected at least twelve flaws, allaying any suspicions he had that good spirits might have been involved in the building of the barn.

'OK!' he told himself. 'Let the show begin!'

The devil then adopted his meditation posture, floating about a foot off the ground with his arms spread wide. Right at that moment, the real Reverend Semmelmeier inside him woke up. 'Help! Help! Someone help me!' The scream took the devil by surprise and came out of his mouth before he could stop it. He focused intensely on the reverend's spirit inside him.

'Sleep .... sleeeeep .... you obnoxious idiot,' he growled. 'Sleeeeep.'

This was the moment Michaela struck. From out of the bushes charged a large rhinoceros, which rammed the floating devil in the back. Incredibly, the devil wasn't sent flying by the colossal impact ... but he did lurch forward several feet ... just enough for his whole body to enter the trap set by Michaela, with the exception of one arm, which hung out of the trap's perimeter.

Having successfully put the Reverend Semmelmeier inside him back to sleep, the devil came out of his meditative state. He instantly detected a shining blue light in his spirit scan and saw that it was emanating from Andy, who had removed his jacket on Michaela's orders.

'Kunnikunde! Kill that boy!' the devil screeched.

The countess, who had been loitering at the entrance looking for an opportunity to strike, reacted within seconds. She launched her iron fist through the open front door across several tables at Andy, who had no chance of avoiding the deadly missile rocketing towards his head.

Outside, Michaela saw what was happening and acted in a split second, magnetising a large steel pillar beside Andy. It diverted Kunnikunde's iron fist, which crashed into it with massive force, punching a jagged hole in the pillar that trapped her fist and held it fast. Fortunately for Kunnikunde, this time there was no liquid manure spewing out of the hole made by her fist. Her extended arm lay loose across several tables between where she was standing at the front entrance and the magnetised pillar inside.

Shocked and enraged, the countess desperately tried to wrench the fist out of the pillar without success. As she violently pulled her loose, stretched arm, it snapped tight like a steel cable, forcefully knocking Lady Heger-Steel's head face-first into a huge bowl of potato salad and sending most of its creamy, lumpy contents flying. Poor Mr Broombridge, who was sitting directly opposite Lady Heger-Steel, took the brunt of the catapulted mix of potatoes, mayonnaise, yogurt, eggs, onion and other ingredients. The bulk of it came to rest in his hair, on his face, all over his suede jacket and in his lap.

'My jacket! My beautiful jacket!' he wailed, after wiping his eyes and looking down at his clothes. 'It's ruined! Why me? Why always me?' He sunk his head in his hands and wept.

Kunnikunde, still struggling to free her iron fist from the pillar yanked her arm so hard that she herself was jolted loose instead of the fist. She became airborne, flying into the barn with considerable speed. Lady Heger-Steel, having extricated her face from the bowl of potato salad, was fiercely casting round trying to identify the guilty party. The flying Countess Kunnikunde, approaching at speed from behind, planted her big moon boot in the middle of Lady Heger-Steel's broad back, thrusting her face into the cucumber salad.

Poor Mr Broombridge was once again the recipient of a flying salad, just, as it happened, at the precise moment he removed his hands from his face after recovering from his bout of weeping.

'You horrible, horrible witch!' Broombridge shouted, either at Lady Heger-Steel or the airborne countess.

The countess wasn't airborne a split second later when she crashed into a large ceiling beam and fell in a heap on the floor. Her iron fist had broken off its extendable arm and dropped down inside the steel pillar. Now restored to her usual self, Kunnikunde was instantly recognisable to Lady Heger-Steel as she lifted her head out of the pile of cucumber salad on the table. The big shiny bowl that originally contained the salad was now perched on her head like a helmet.

'You!' Lady Heger-Steel shouted, glaring fiercely at the dazed countess who was dragging herself painfully to her feet.

Then Lady Heger-Steel spotted Mr Broombridge, who had made two tactical errors. One: he should have kept his hands covering his face. And two: he shouldn't have shouted, 'You horrible, horrible witch!'

'And you!' Lady Heger-Steel shrieked at him. 'The pervert!'

The word 'pervert' was now an instant alarm signal for Broombridge. He dropped his crutch and started running ... well, it was more a frantic, panic-stricken hobbling, actually. He was closely followed by a still dazed and bruised Kunnikunde, who was more stumbling at speed rather than running in its strictest, technical sense. Hot on their heels was Lady Heger-Steel, who was doing a convincing impression of the rhinoceros that had earlier charged the devil.

Somehow Kunnikunde and Broombridge reached his car ahead of the lady rhinoceros, who was closing rapidly, snorting and whistling with anger and outrage, the empty cucumber salad bowl still firmly wedged on her head.

They both jumped into the car and locked the doors.

'Drive! Drive!' Kunnikunde screeched.

But Mr Broombridge, being typically Teutonian, first had to fasten his seatbelt and get the feel of his steering wheel before pressing the starter button. By this time, Lady Heger-Steel was banging the huge fist of one hand on the driver's window and trying to rip the door open with the other.

When Broombridge finally pushed the starter button, he thought he must have jumped into a rocket instead of his car. It was the last thought he had before waking up some time later in a hospital bed with his passenger in the bed opposite him.

Mr Broombridge and the evil countess had had no idea, of course, that Dr Folterknecht's temporarily miniaturised armoured vehicle was right under their limousine. When the tiny armoured vehicle suddenly zapped back to its normal size, it had catapulted Broombridge's car high into the air before it crashed-landed upside down in the forest, wedging itself between two trees, with its two passengers out for the count.

As with all big events, there was an ambulance already in attendance. However, in this case, it wasn't nearly enough. The fire brigade and a police rescue team had to be called to cut the two passengers from the twisted wreck and extricate them from the tree branches. Only then was the ambulance employed to rush Kunnikunde and Mr Broombridge to the hospital.

28

Restored to normal size along with his armoured car, Dr Folterknecht could hear a loud banging. He opened the hatch and stuck his head out. When he saw Lady Heger-Steel furiously thumping the side of his vehicle with her fist, he shouted, 'Stop hitting my car, you monstrous cow!'

The catapulting of Mr Broombridge's limo had happened too quickly for Lady Heger-Steel to realise at first that the vehicle she was attacking wasn't the limousine at all.

Dr Folterknecht's offensive insult instantly cleared her head. The doctor himself was unsuccessfully trying to raise the dart machine gun mounted beside the hatch, but the impact of his vehicle thrusting Broombridge's limo skywards seemed to have jammed it. He didn't realise the gun had been sabotaged by Andy ramming a metal bar into its mechanism.

Lady Heger-Steel pulled the salad bowl from her head and launched it at the head of Dr Folterknecht, still sticking out of the hatch as he struggled with the dart gun. The force of the bowl flattened the doctor's nose and stunned him momentarily. His assailant ran around to get to him from the other side and give him a solid thumping.

At that moment the devil, who was caught in Michaela's trap, spotted Andy near the armoured car. His one free arm still outside the trap shot towards Andy in an attempt to grab him and pull him close. Andy wouldn't have seen it coming except that in her rush to get to Folterknecht, Lady Heger-Steel got in the way of the devil's arm for a second, giving Andy time to clutch onto the armoured car before the devil's hand got a grip on him. Andy powerfully resisted, surprising the devil, who was unaware of Andy's super strength gifted to him by the magic pencil. Their respective strengths were evenly matched, and the devil began to pull Andy and the armoured car towards him.

By this time, Dr Folterknecht was no longer in his armoured car. He had been dragged out of it by the 'monstrous cow,' as he had foolishly called Lady Heger-Steel, who now had him on the ground steadily belting him.

Sometimes, when humans are in trouble, their best friend can be their dog. Folterknecht didn't have a dog, but Andy did ... and what a dog! Sassy suddenly grew to the size of a bull elephant and savagely bit into the devil's arm. Her enormous teeth flashed with a blue spark and severed his arm. A mightily relieved Andy shook himself free of the devil's grip and flung the severed arm away in disgust. 'Uughhh—Yuk!' he yelled, screwing up his face.

The severed arm landed on the ground right beside the battered face of Dr Folterknecht, who was barely conscious after his fearsome belting at the hands of Lady Heger-Steel. She had finally desisted and stormed off, feeling that justice had been done.

The sight of the disgusting arm on the ground beside him revived the pummeled doctor somewhat. 'A part of an alien!' he croaked. 'My proof, at last!' Grabbing the hideous arm, Folterknecht managed to crawl back into the armoured car with it. Ignoring the pain from his crushed nose and battered head, he switched the vehicle into flight mode and started to slowly and carefully lift off in the narrow space between the two catering trucks.

Immobilised in his trap, the one-armed devil was screaming, 'Kill! Kill! Everybody, kill!'

Responding at once, the five secret policemen under his spell stormed into the barn with guns drawn, followed closely by Werner Little Werner. But they didn't get a chance to shoot anybody. The second they entered the barn, the magic that Michaela had infused into the building's structure cleansed them of any evil spells. They simply stood together in a stupor, looking totally confused. Seconds later the loud clattering of propellers rattled them out of their stupor, and they started remembering what their real mission was.

'Folterknecht!' officer Karl-Otto yelled.

As one, the five secret police raced out of the barn towards the two big catering trucks.

'Too late!' Karl-Otto cried, as Folterknecht's flying machine hovered above the trucks and was starting to move off. Karl-Otto managed to get one shotgun blast into the underside of the flying machine, producing a single scream of pain from Folterknecht, before he flew away across the forest, heading north.

The policemen rushed up to Werner, who was wandering around wondering what had happened to his master, the devil.

'Mr Little Werner,' Karl-Otto said. 'Please drive us immediately to the big city airport. We need a plane to chase Dr Folterknecht.'

'Absolutely not!' Werner cried. 'I am looking for my master. I cannot leave here without his permission!'

A second later, five police pistols aimed at his head convinced Werner that he didn't need his master's permission after all.

At the airport, the secret police officers commandeered a plane and chased Folterknecht to their headquarters where the mad doctor was taking the devil's severed arm as proof that aliens existed.

When he first arrived, none of his former colleagues recognised him, mainly because of his severe facial bruising and remodelled nose, squashed flat by the heavy cucumber salad bowl Lady Heger-Steel had thrown at him. They wouldn't have recognised him from behind either because his backside was extremely swollen due to two lots of shotgun pellets embedded in it. The first lot was courtesy of farmer Dungenfeld, who had quite accurately fired a load of them into Folterknecht's behind as the doctor flew over his field on the way to the party. The second lot was delivered just as accurately by Karl-Otto's service-issued shotgun.

The secret police authorities immediately threw Dr Folterknecht into jail, dismissing his alien arm claim as complete nonsense.

29

When Werner had sped off to the big city airport with the five secret policemen on board, he was unaware that his master, the devil, had now come to the shocking realisation that he couldn't escape what he thought was only a junior spirit trap. He furiously tried to smash his way out with a lot of howling and screeching, which somehow wasn't heard by the revellers in the barn, who were having a great time eating, drinking and dancing to the music of the oompah band.

'Release me, immediately!' the devil reverend screamed at Michaela and Andy, who had just joined her next to the trap. 'If you do not, I will turn your life into misery for the next twenty years!'

The angrier and more animated the devil reverend got, the less control he had over the real Reverend Semmelmeier's body, which was waking up more often. When the devil made an even more violent attempt to break out of the trap, the reverend was suddenly wide awake. Now of no use to him, the devil stepped out of Semmelmeier's body. As he did so, the reverend fell out of the trap and lay motionless on the ground. Quickly the pencil acted and magically restored the reverend's severed arm.

Free of the human body, the devil was once again in his usual form of a hideous creature. To Andy, he seemed to be some kind of horrendous half-humanoid, half-beast with the head of an unbelievably ugly and vicious dog. Andy thought the devil looked like a werewolf ... but a particularly ugly and terrifying one.

Sassy, now returned to her normal size, jumped between the devil and Andy, barking ferociously, ready to defend her master to the death.

'Release me!' the hideous creature screamed again.

'Never! I won't release you!' Andy cried, sounding braver than he felt.

'Lucifer,' Michaela said calmly, 'I believe that's your name. First, I want you to release the three spirits you have trapped in your mirror. Only then will I be prepared to negotiate.'

'Who are you ... you filthy little human?' the devil spat. 'You dare talk to me? ... Lucifer ... the King of Darkness! Those spirits will stay in my mirror for all of eternity! They will be my most precious trophies! Now, get me the vile spirit that put me in this ridiculous trap before I have to smash through it.' His pulsing red eyes bored into Andy's with sheer evil and hate. 'And you, foul boy ... next time we meet I will suck all your powers out of you and leave you a rotting vegetable!'

'No, you won't!' Michaela retorted. 'Not if I do this!'

She touched Andy's hand and a pink flash shimmered over his whole body, then disappeared.

At this, the devil went truly berserk. He grew to ten times his normal size; so did Michaela. She very slowly removed her jacket to reveal her true form to the devil.

Andy was gobsmacked. *She really does look like a guardian angel!* he thought.

The devil howled, incandescent with rage. With Michaela's cloaking device gone, the devil realised that he had been tricked by a powerful good spirit. She was glowing bright red in his scan and Andy a bright pink.

'You have given a human being divine powers!' the devil hissed at Michaela. 'That is against all the rules of the spirit universe!'

'For us, there is only one rule,' Michaela replied, 'that good must prevail over evil! Now, release those three spirits from your mirror ... or do I have to do it myself?'

'You can't! You can't!' the devil screeched with laughter. But a second later his laughter evaporated. 'No! Oh no!' he screamed as his mirror started pulsing bright red and then exploded.

Three bright blue lights circulated around Michaela's head several times, like floating stars, as if they were saying thank you, then vanished into thin air. Suddenly three massive creatures like dolphins, with kind eyes and large mouths, grabbed the devil from the trap. Just as suddenly, in the blink of an eye, all were gone.

Michaela resumed her normal size and attended to Reverend Semmelmeier, who was moaning and groaning on the ground.

'I saw an angel!' he stammered.

'Andy, carry the reverend into the barn,' Michaela ordered.

Lifting him easily with his greatly increased strength, Andy carried the reverend inside to the party where he soon recovered completely and joined in the fun.

'Nobody remembers the nights they got lots of sleep, Count Johann!' someone exclaimed. 'I won't forget tonight in a hurry! What a party!'

Several other voices cheered their agreement. It seemed no one wanted to go home; the festivities went on well into the night.

It helped that none of the revellers inside the barn had a clue about what had been going on outside. Only Commander Wurstling got a belated glimpse of it when he inspected the wreck of Mr Broombridge's limousine. 'Reckless parking in the forest!' he concluded.

Unavoidably, Johann had to endure several speeches. The one he would have most preferred to avoid was given by Rollover von Cracklingen, Andy's uncle and loyal ally of his Aunt Kunnikunde.

'All I'm interested in is having peace in the family,' an obviously inebriated Rollover declared.

Johann didn't believe it for a second. But in the spirit of the evening, he listened politely. The truth was, he felt totally betrayed by that side of his family. However, knowing their laziness, snobbishness and complete incompetence in all aspects of running a business, he started to feel sorry for them.

Magnanimously, he shook Rollover's hand after his speech but still made his feelings clear. 'There will never be peace in the family, Rollover, until Countess Kunnikunde stays out of our lives.'

Rollover started to argue the point, but a long line of people pushing forward to talk with Johann cut him short, and he wobbled off to top up his glass yet again.

30

One of the happiest people at the party seemed to be Michaela, who was smiling all night. Andy could understand why she was so pleased with herself; her plan had succeeded so well.

When Johann's big party finally wound up, he, Anna, Andy and Michaela were the last to leave. Arriving home exhausted but very happy, they all went straight to bed. The moment Michaela was in Andy's bedroom, she changed back into the magic pencil. Andy wasn't quite ready to go to sleep; he was desperate to know what had happened to the devil.

'He was transported far away and is being guarded by good spirits who come from the planet Orka,' the pencil answered, once again just a voice in Andy's head. 'They should be able to keep him trapped for about four or five years. Eventually though, he will escape, assisted by his dark spirits.'

'Won't he then come after us?' Andy asked, wide-eyed.

''Oh, yes, he will,' the pencil answered calmly. 'Once he is free, he will try three more times to destroy you.'

Andy emitted an anguished gasp.

'He will hire trained assassins from another planet,' the pencil continued, matter-of-factly, 'and send them to Earth to hunt you down. These assassins are extremely dangerous, to say the least. They have even less humour than your nasty Aunt Kunnikunde, but also possess what you would call superpowers.

'Of course, your Aunt Kunnikunde will also make other attempts to kill you. And so will certain others. So, for the next few years, you will have to train every day! You will need to be fully focused and committed to mastering the gifts I have given you. That is your only chance to survive and grow up to be a respected and proud man like your father.'

'Why me?' Andy wailed. 'Why is everyone after me?'

'Do I hear self-pity?' the pencil scolded. 'Being empowered with vast knowledge, is that so bad? Having the ability to pass any exam without having to study and do homework? That must be terrible for you! Teleporting? Telehopping through walls and doors? Being, already, the strongest and fastest human being on your planet, able to leap the highest mountain in the world and land softly on your feet with the anti-gravity gift I've given you? I'm feeling really sorry for you!'

'Stop! Stop!' Andy cried. 'That was not what I meant! What I was really trying to say was, why me and not somebody else?'

'The answer to that question you won't find out until after you die,' the pencil said gently. 'In the meantime, you should feel privileged at having been chosen, and try to live life to the fullest. There will be failure, betrayal and hurt. But without them, you will never know what happiness is all about.'

Andy simply nodded. His brain was processing so much information and emotion that for a few moments he was unable to say anything. But as he slowly gathered his thoughts, he told himself that self-pity led to nothing and that he was indeed privileged and had to develop an attitude worthy of it.

'Bring it on! he blurted out. 'Whatever happens, I'll try to handle it!'

31

The least happy people the night of the party were Kunnikunde and poor Mr Broombridge. Both woke up in hospital beds fully bandaged and fitted with neck braces. In addition to broken arms and severe bruising, the evil countess suffered a massive concussion. As a result, she temporarily lost all recollection of her recent past and was quite pleasant for a while.

With Kunnikunde in the hospital, Mr Werner Little Werner systematically stole all the huge bags of money Kunnikunde had accumulated at her castle at Stone. He fled with it to a faraway country and changed his name. But he lived in fear of Kunnikunde's murderous wrath, knowing she wouldn't give up until she had killed him.

When the countess was released from the hospital and found out her precious money had been stolen, her anger attacks went off the scale. She ended up in a mental hospital for a long time. Two or three times every day she was heard screaming, 'I will find you, Werner! I will punish you! And then I will kill you!'

Mr Broombridge, following his release from the hospital, returned to the old Ritter von Krumm pencil factory and rejoined his fellow board members, Rollover von Cracklingen and Farty von Krumm. Together they continued their unfinished work of tarnishing the once famous and respected brand of their factory's pencil products. In stark contrast, however, next door Johann's pencil business was going from strength to strength.

Dr Folterknecht left the mental hospital just as Kunnikunde was entering it. The severed limb the doctor had given to the secret police underwent rigorous scientific testing. To their astonishment, the tests confirmed that the gruesome arm was not human and not from any other earthly creature. The inescapable conclusion was that it was indeed alien of some kind.

On the strength of this finding, the secret police cautiously allowed that maybe, just maybe, Folterknecht wasn't insane after all. There was enough doubt in their minds to release him from incarceration and summon him to a meeting with the top military generals, as well as the defence minister himself.

Dr Folterknecht was on his best behaviour at the meeting and kept his insanity well-hidden and under control. It was decided that a new department should be established, with Folterknecht in charge, to investigate unexplained phenomena.

The doctor started his new duties the very next day, rubbing his hands together with extreme satisfaction and excitement. He was obsessively thorough and focused with his investigations. It wasn't until almost five years later that he was finally able to act on his findings and reappeared in Stone, accompanied by a considerable force of secret police commandoes. His targets were a teenage boy and girl, Reverend Semmelmeier and, of course, the greedy and evil Countess Kunnikunde.

Thankfully, Andy was prepared. The magic pencil had put together a rigorous training schedule for him. Though the spirit of the magic pencil was often away, sometimes for months on end, preparing for its own part in the next journey, Andy kept up his part of the bargain by sticking to it with enthusiasm and determination. So, when something unexpected and extraordinary happened ... but that's another story.

Illustrations by Caroline Webb

www.ingramcontent.com/pod-product-compliance
Lightning Source LLC
LaVergne TN
LVHW011718060526
838200LV00051B/2945